TEHANU

First Paperback edition September 2001

Copyright © 1990 by Ursula K. Le Guin

Simon Pulse Paperbacks

An imprint of Simon & Schuster Children's Publishing Division

1230 Avenue of the Americas, New York, NY 10020

All rights reserved, including the right of reproduction in whole or in part in any form.

Also available in an Atheneum Books for Young Readers edition.

Designed by Debra Sfetsios

The text of this book was set in Adobe Garamond.

Printed in the United States of America.   10 9 8 7 6 5 4 3 2 1

Library of Congress Control Number 89-32780 (hardcover edition)

ISBN 0-689-84533-2

URSULA K. LE GUIN

TEHANU

A Jean Karl Book

SIMON PULSE

NEW YORK LONDON TORONTO SYDNEY SINGAPORE

Contents

A Bad Thing
1

Going to the Falcon's Nest
7

Ogion
22

Kalessin
34

Bettering
55

Worsening
82

Mice
95

Hawks
116

Finding Words
139

The Dolphin
161

Home
183

Winter
221

The Master
251

Tehanu
272

Only in silence the word,
only in dark the light,
only in dying life:
bright the hawk's flight
on the empty sky.

—*The Creation of Éa*

A Bad Thing

AFTER FARMER FLINT OF THE MIDDLE Valley died, his widow stayed on at the farmhouse. Her son had gone to sea and her daughter had married a merchant of Valmouth, so she lived alone at Oak Farm. People said she had been some kind of great person in the foreign land she came from, and indeed the mage Ogion used to stop by Oak Farm to see her; but that didn't count for much, since Ogion visited all sorts of nobodies.

She had a foreign name, but Flint had called her Goha, which is what they call a little white web-spinning spider on Gont. That name fit well enough, she being white-skinned and small and a good spinner of goat's-wool and sheep-fleece. So now she was Flint's widow, Goha, mistress of a flock of sheep and the land to pasture them, four fields, an orchard of pears, two tenants' cottages, the old stone farmhouse under the oaks, and the family graveyard over the hill where Flint lay, earth in his earth.

"I've generally lived near tombstones," she said to her daughter.

"Oh, mother, come live in town with us!" said Apple, but the widow would not leave her solitude.

"Maybe later, when there are babies and you'll need a hand," she said, looking with pleasure at her grey-eyed daughter. "But not now. You don't need me. And I like it here."

When Apple had gone back to her young husband, the widow closed the door and stood on the stone-flagged floor of the kitchen of the farmhouse. It was dusk, but she did not light the lamp, thinking of her own husband lighting the lamp: the hands, the spark, the intent, dark face in the catching glow. The house was silent.

"I used to live in a silent house, alone," she thought. "I will do so again." She lighted the lamp.

In a late afternoon of the first hot weather, the widow's old friend Lark came out from the village, hurrying along the dusty lane. "Goha," she said, seeing her weeding in the bean patch, "Goha, it's a bad thing. It's a very bad thing. Can you come?"

"Yes," the widow said. "What would the bad thing be?"

Lark caught her breath. She was a heavy, plain, middle-aged woman, whose name did not fit her body any more. But once she had been a slight and pretty girl, and she had befriended Goha, paying no attention to the villagers who gossiped about that white-faced Kargish witch Flint had brought home; and friends they had been ever since.

"A burned child," she said.

"Whose?"

"Tramps'."

Goha went to shut the farmhouse door, and they set off along the lane, Lark talking as they went. She was short of breath and sweating. Tiny seeds of the heavy grasses that lined the lane stuck to her cheeks and forehead, and she brushed at them as she talked. "They've been camped in the river meadows all the month. A man, passed himself off as a tinker, but he's a thief, and a woman with him. And another man, younger, hanging around with them most of the time. Not working, any of 'em. Filching and begging and living off the woman. Boys from downriver were bringing them farmstuff to get at her. You know how it is now, that kind of thing. And gangs on the roads and coming by farms. If I were you, I'd lock my door, these days. So this one, this younger fellow, comes into the village, and I was out in front of our house, and he says, 'The child's not well.' I'd barely seen a child with them, a little ferret of a thing, slipped out of sight so quick I wasn't sure it was there at all. So I said, 'Not well? A fever?' And the fellow says, 'She hurt herself, lighting the fire,' and then before I'd got myself ready to go with him he'd made off. Gone. And when I went out there by the river, the other pair was gone too. Cleared out. Nobody. All their traps and trash gone too. There was just their campfire, still smoldering, and just by it—partly in it—on the ground—"

Lark stopped talking for several steps. She looked straight ahead, not at Goha.

"They hadn't even put a blanket over her," she said.

She strode on.

"She'd been pushed into the fire while it was burning," she said. She swallowed, and brushed at the sticking seeds on her hot face. "I'd say maybe she fell, but if she'd been awake she'd have tried to save herself. They beat her and thought they'd killed her, I guess, and wanted to hide what they'd done to her, so they—"

She stopped again, went on again.

"Maybe it wasn't him. Maybe he pulled her out. He came to get help for her, after all. It must have been the father. I don't know. It doesn't matter. Who's to know? Who's to care? Who's to care for the child? Why do we do what we do?"

Goha asked in a low voice, "Will she live?"

"She might," Lark said. "She might well live."

After a while, as they neared the village, she said, "I don't know why I had to come to you. Ivy's there. There's nothing to be done."

"I could go to Valmouth, for Beech."

"Nothing he could do. It's beyond . . . beyond

help. I got her warm. Ivy's given her a potion and a sleeping charm. I carried her home. She must be six or seven but she didn't weigh what a two-year-old would. She never really waked. But she makes a sort of gasping. . . . I know there isn't anything you can do. But I wanted you."

"I want to come," Goha said. But before they entered Lark's house, she shut her eyes and held her breath a moment in dread.

Lark's children had been sent outdoors, and the house was silent. The child lay unconscious on Lark's bed. The village witch, Ivy, had smeared an ointment of witch hazel and heal-all on the lesser burns, but had not touched the right side of the face and head and the right hand, which had been charred to the bone. She had drawn the rune Pirr above the bed, and left it at that.

"Can you do anything?" Lark asked in a whisper.

Goha stood looking down at the burned child. Her hands were still. She shook her head.

"You learned healing, up on the mountain, didn't you?" Pain and shame and rage spoke through Lark, begging for relief.

"Even Ogion couldn't heal this," the widow said.

Lark turned away, biting her lip, and wept. Goha held her, stroking her grey hair. They held each other.

The witch Ivy came in from the kitchen, scowling at the sight of Goha. Though the widow cast no charms and worked no spells, it was said that when she first came to Gont she had lived at Re Albi as a ward of the mage, and that she knew the Archmage of Roke, and no doubt had foreign and uncanny powers. Jealous of her prerogative, the witch went to the bed and busied herself beside it, making a mound of something in a dish and setting it afire so that it smoked and reeked while she muttered a curing charm over and over. The rank herbal smoke made the burned child cough and half rouse, flinching and shuddering. She began to make a gasping noise, quick, short, scraping breaths. Her one eye seemed to look up at Goha.

Goha stepped forward and took the child's left hand in hers. She spoke in her own language. "I served them and I left them," she said. "I will not let them have you."

The child stared at her or at nothing, trying to breathe, and trying again to breathe, and trying again to breathe.

GOING TO THE FALCON'S NEST

IT WAS MORE THAN A YEAR LATER, in the hot and spacious days after the Long Dance, that a messenger came down the road from the north to Middle Valley asking for the widow Goha. People in the village put him on the path, and he came to Oak Farm late in the afternoon. He was a sharp-faced, quick-eyed man. He looked at Goha and at the sheep in the fold beyond her and said, "Fine lambs. The Mage of Re Albi sends for you."

"He sent you?" Goha inquired, disbelieving and amused. Ogion, when he wanted her, had quicker and finer messengers: an eagle calling, or only his own voice saying her name quietly—*Will you come?*

The man nodded. "He's sick," he said. "Will you be selling off any of the ewe lambs?"

"I might. You can talk to the shepherd if you like. Over by the fence there. Do you want supper? You can stay the night here if you want, but I'll be on my way."

"Tonight?"

This time there was no amusement in her look of mild scorn. "I won't be waiting about," she said. She spoke for a minute with the old shepherd, Clearbrook, and then turned away, going up to the house built into the hillside by the oak grove. The messenger followed her.

In the stone-floored kitchen, a child whom he looked at once and quickly looked away from served him milk, bread, cheese, and green onions, and then went off, never saying a word. She reappeared beside the woman, both shod for travel and carrying light leather packs. The messenger followed them out, and the widow locked the farmhouse door. They all set off together, he on his business, for the message from Ogion had been a mere favor added to the serious matter of buying a breeding ram for the Lord of Re Albi; and the woman and the burned child bade him farewell where the lane turned off to the village. They went on up the road he had come down, northward and then west into the foothills of Gont Mountain.

They walked until the long summer twilight began to darken. They left the narrow road then and made camp in a dell down by a stream that ran quick and quiet, reflecting the pale evening sky between thickets of scrub willow. Goha made a bed of dry grass and willow leaves, hidden among the thickets like a hare's form, and rolled the child up in a blanket on it. "Now," she said, "you're a cocoon. In the morning you'll be a butterfly and hatch out." She lighted no fire, but lay in her cloak beside the child and watched the stars shine one by one and listened to what the stream said quietly, until she slept.

When they woke in the cold before the dawn, she made a small fire and heated a pan of water to make oatmeal gruel for the child and herself. The little ruined butterfly came shivering from her cocoon, and Goha cooled the pan in the dewy grass so that the child could hold it and drink from it. The east was brightening above the high, dark shoulder of the mountain when they set off again.

They walked all day at the pace of a child who tired easily. The woman's heart yearned to make haste, but she walked slowly. She was not able to carry the child any long distance, and so to make the way easier for her she told her stories.

"We're going to see a man, an old man, called Ogion," she told her as they trudged along the narrow road that wound upward through the forests. "He's a wise man, and a wizard. Do you know what a wizard is, Therru?"

If the child had had a name, she did not know it or would not say it. Goha called her Therru.

She shook her head.

"Well, neither do I," said the woman. "But I know what they can do. When I was young—older than you, but young—Ogion was my father, the way I'm your mother now. He looked after me and tried to teach me what I needed to know. He stayed with me when he'd rather have been wandering by himself. He liked to walk, all along these roads like we're doing now, and in the forests, in the wild places. He went everywhere on the mountain, looking at things, listening. He always listened, so they called him the Silent. But he used to talk to me. He told me stories. Not only the great stories everybody learns, the heroes and the kings and the things that happened long ago and far away, but stories only he knew." She walked on a way before she went on. "I'll tell you one of those stories now.

"One of the things wizards can do is turn into something else—take another form. Shape-changing, they call it. An ordinary sorcerer can make himself look like somebody else, or like an animal, just so you don't know for a minute what you're seeing—as if he'd put on a mask. But the wizards and mages can do more than that. They can be the mask, they can truly change into another being. So a wizard, if he wanted to cross the sea and had no boat, might turn himself into a gull and fly across. But he has to be careful. If he stays a bird, he begins to think what a bird thinks and forget what a man thinks, and he might fly off and be a gull and never a man again. So they say there was a great wizard once who liked to turn himself into a bear, and did it too often, and became a bear, and killed his own little son; and they had to hunt him down and kill him. But Ogion used to joke about it, too. Once when the mice got into his pantry and ruined the cheese, he caught one with a tiny mousetrap spell, and he held the mouse up like this and looked it in the eye and said, 'I told you not to play mouse!' And for a minute I thought he meant it. . . .

"Well, this story is about something like shape-changing, but Ogion said it was beyond all shape-changing he knew, because it was about being two things, two beings, at once, and in the same form, and he said that this is beyond the power of wizards. But he met with it in a little village around on the northwest coast of Gont, a place called Kemay. There was a woman there, an old fisherwoman, not a witch, not learned; but she made songs. That's how Ogion came to hear of her. He was wandering there, the way he did, going along the coast, listening; and he heard somebody singing, mending a net or caulking a boat and singing as they worked:

> *Farther west than west*
> *beyond the land*
> *my people are dancing*
> *on the other wind.*

"It was the tune and the words both that Ogion heard, and he had never heard them before, so he asked where the song came from. And from one answer to another, he went along to where somebody said, 'Oh, that's one of the songs of the Woman of Kemay.' So he went on along to Kemay, the little fishing port where the woman lived, and he found her house down by the harbor. And he knocked on the door with his mage's staff. And she came and opened the door.

"Now you know, you remember when we talked about names, how children have child-names, and everybody has a use-name, and maybe a nickname too. Different people may call you differently. You're my Therru, but maybe you'll have a Hardic use-name when you get older. But also, when you come into your womanhood, you will, if all be rightly done, be given your true name. It will be given you by one of true power, a wizard or a mage, because that is their power, their art—naming. And that's the name you'll maybe never tell another person, because your own self is in your true name. It is your strength, your power; but to another it is risk and burden, only to be given in utmost need and trust. But a great mage, knowing all names, may know it without your telling him.

"So Ogion, who is a great mage, stood at the door of the little house there by the seawall, and the old woman opened the door. Then Ogion stepped back, and he held up his oak staff, and put up his hand, too, like this, as if trying to protect himself from the heat of a fire, and in his amazement and fear he said her true name aloud—'Dragon!'

"In that first moment, he told me, it was no woman he saw at all in the doorway, but a blaze and glory of fire, and a glitter of gold scales and talons, and the great eyes of a dragon. They say you must not look into a dragon's eyes.

"Then that was gone, and he saw no dragon, but an old woman standing there in the doorway, a bit stooped, a tall old fisherwoman with big hands. She looked at him as he did at her. And she said, 'Come in, Lord Ogion.'

"So he went in. She served him fish soup, and they ate, and then they talked by her fire. He thought that she must be a shape-changer, but he didn't know, you see, whether she was a woman who could change herself into a dragon, or a dragon who could change itself into a woman. So he asked her at last, 'Are you woman or dragon?' And she didn't say, but she said, 'I'll sing you a story I know.'"

Therru had a little stone in her shoe. They stopped to get that out, and went on, very slowly, for the road was climbing steeply between cut banks of stone overhung by thickets where the cicadas sang in the summer heat.

"So this is the story she sang to him, to Ogion.

"When Segoy raised the islands of the world from the sea in the beginning of time, the dragons were the first born of the land and the wind blowing over the land. So the Song of the Creation tells. But her song told also that then, in the beginning, dragon and human were all one. They were all one people, one race, winged, and speaking the True Language.

"They were beautiful, and strong, and wise, and free.

"But in time nothing can be without becoming. So among the dragon-people some became more and more in love with flight and wildness, and would have less and less to do with the works of making, or with study and learning, or with houses and cities. They wanted only to fly farther and farther, hunting and eating their kill, ignorant and uncaring, seeking more freedom and more.

"Others of the dragon-people came to care little for flight, but gathered up treasure, wealth, things made, things learned. They built houses, strongholds to keep their treasures in, so they could pass all they gained to their children, ever seeking more increase and more. And they came to fear the wild ones, who might come flying and destroy all their dear hoard, burn it up in a blast of flame out of mere carelessness and ferocity.

"The wild ones feared nothing. They learned nothing. Because they were ignorant and fearless, they could not save themselves when the flightless ones trapped them as animals and killed them. But other wild ones would come flying and set the beautiful houses afire, and destroy, and kill. Those that were strongest, wild or wise, were those who killed each other first.

"Those who were most afraid, they hid from the fighting, and when there was no more hiding they ran from it. They used their skills of making and made boats and sailed east, away from the western isles where the great winged ones made war among the ruined towers.

"So those who had been both dragon and human changed, becoming two peoples—the dragons, always fewer and wilder, scattered by their endless, mindless greed and anger, in the far islands of the Western Reach; and the human folk, always more numerous in their rich towns and cities, filling up the Inner Isles and all the south and east. But among them there were some who saved the learning of the dragons—the True Language of the Making—and these are now the wizards.

"But also, the song said, there are those among us who know they once were dragons, and among the dragons there are some who know their kinship with us. And these say that when the one people were becoming two, some of them, still both human and dragon, still winged, went not east but west, on over the Open Sea, till they came to the other side of the world. There they live in peace, great winged beings both wild and wise, with human mind and dragon heart. And so she sang,

Farther west than west
beyond the land
my people are dancing
on the other wind.

"So that was the story told in the song of the Woman of Kemay, and it ended with those words.

"Then Ogion said to her, 'When I first saw you I saw your true being. This woman who sits across the hearth from me is no more than the dress she wears.'

"But she shook her head and laughed, and all she would say was, 'If only it were that simple!'

"So then after a while Ogion came back to Re Albi. And when he told me the story, he said to me, 'Ever since that day, I have wondered if anyone, man or dragon, has been farther west than west; and who we are, and where our wholeness lies.' . . . Are you getting hungry, Therru? There's a good sitting place, it looks like, up there where the road turns. Maybe from there we'll be able to see Gont Port, away down at the foot of the mountain. It's a big city, even bigger than Valmouth. We'll sit down when we get to the turn, and rest a bit."

From the high corner of the road they could indeed look down the vast slopes of forest and rocky meadow to the town on its bay, and see the crags that guarded the entrance to the bay, and the boats on the dark water like wood-chips or water beetles. Far ahead on their road and still somewhat above it, a cliff jutted out from the mountainside: the Overfell, on which was the village of Re Albi, the Falcon's Nest.

Therru made no complaints, but when presently Goha said, "Well, shall we go on?" the child, sitting there between the road and the gulfs of sky and sea, shook her head. The sun was warm, and they had walked a long way since their breakfast in the dell.

Goha brought out their water bottle, and they drank again; then she brought out a bag of raisins and walnuts and gave it to the child.

"We're in sight of where we're going," she said, "and I'd like to be there before dark, if we can. I'm anxious to see Ogion. You'll be very tired, but we won't walk fast. And we'll be there safe and warm tonight. Keep the bag, tuck it in your belt. Raisins make your legs strong. Would you like a staff—like a wizard—to help you walk?"

Therru munched and nodded. Goha took out her knife and cut a strong shoot of hazel for the child, and then seeing an alder fallen above the road, broke off a branch of it and trimmed it to make herself a stout, light stick.

They set off again, and the child trudged along, beguiled by raisins. Goha sang to amuse them both, love songs and shepherd's songs and ballads she had learned in the Middle Valley; but all at once her voice hushed in the middle of a tune. She stopped, putting out her hand in a warning gesture.

The four men ahead of them on the road had seen her. There was no use trying to hide in the woods till they went on or went by.

"Travelers," she said quietly to Therru, and walked on. She took a good grip on her alder stick.

What Lark had said about gangs and thieves was not just the complaint each generation makes that things aren't what they used to be and the world's going to the dogs. In the last several years there had been a loss of peace and trust in the towns and countrysides of Gont. Young men behaved like strangers among their own people, abusing hospitality, stealing, selling what they stole. Beggary was common where it had been rare, and the unsatisfied beggar threatened violence. Women did not like to go alone in the streets and roads, nor did they like that loss of freedom. Some of the young women ran off to join the gangs of thieves and poachers. Often they came home within the year, sullen, bruised, and pregnant. And among village sorcerers and witches there was rumor of matters of their profession going amiss: charms that had always cured did not cure; spells of finding found nothing, or the wrong thing; love potions drove men into frenzies not of desire but of murderous jealousy. And worse than this, they said, people who knew nothing of the art of magic, the laws and limits of it and the dangers of breaking them, were calling themselves people of power, promising wonders of wealth and health to their followers, promising even immortality.

Ivy, the witch of Goha's village, had spoken darkly of this weakening of magic, and so had Beech, the sorcerer of Valmouth. He was a shrewd and modest man, who had come to help Ivy do what little could be done to lessen the pain and scarring of Therru's burns. He had said to Goha, "I think a time in which such things as this occur must be a time of ruining, the end of an age. How many hundred years since there was a king in Havnor? It can't go on so. We must turn to the center again or be lost, island against island, man against man, father against child. . . ." He had glanced at her, somewhat timidly, yet with his clear, shrewd look. "The Ring of Erreth-Akbe is restored to the Tower in Havnor," he said. "I know who brought it there. . . . That was the sign, surely, that was the sign of the new age to come! But we haven't acted on it. We have no king. We have no center. We must find our heart, our strength. Maybe the Archmage will act at last." And he added, with confidence, "After all, he is from Gont."

But no word of any deed of the Archmage, or any heir to the Throne in Havnor, had come; and things went badly on.

So it was with fear and a grim anger that Goha saw the four men on the road before her step two to each side, so that she and the child would have to pass between them.

As they went walking steadily forward, Therru

kept very close beside her, holding her head bent down, but she did not take her hand.

One of the men, a big-chested fellow with coarse black hairs on his upper lip drooping over his mouth, began to speak, grinning a little. "Hey, there," he said, but Goha spoke at the same time and louder. "Out of my way!" she said, raising her alder stick as if it were a wizard's staff—"I have business with Ogion!" She strode between the men and straight on, Therru trotting beside her. The men, mistaking effrontery for witchery, stood still. Ogion's name perhaps still held power. Or perhaps there was a power in Goha, or in the child. For when the two had gone by, one of the men said, "Did you see that?" and spat and made the sign to avert evil.

"Witch and her monster brat," another said. "Let 'em go!"

Another, a man in a leather cap and jerkin, stood staring for a moment while the others slouched on their way. His face looked sick and stricken, yet he seemed to be turning to follow the woman and child, when the hairy-lipped man called to him, "Come on, Handy!" and he obeyed.

Out of sight around the turn of the road, Goha had picked up Therru and hurried on with her until she had to set her down and stand gasping. The child asked no questions and made no delays. As soon as Goha could go on again, the child walked as fast as she could beside her, holding her hand.

"You're red," she said. "Like fire."

She spoke seldom, and not clearly, her voice being very hoarse; but Goha could understand her.

"I'm angry," Goha said with a kind of laugh. "When I'm angry I turn red. Like you people, you red people, you barbarians of the western lands. . . Look, there's a town there ahead, that'll be Oak Springs. It's the only village on this road. We'll stop there and rest a little. Maybe we can get some milk. And then, if we can go on, if you think you can walk on up to the Falcon's Nest, we'll be there by nightfall, I hope."

The child nodded. She opened her bag of raisins and walnuts and ate a few. They trudged on.

The sun had long set when they came through the village and to Ogion's house on the cliff-top. The first stars glimmered above a dark mass of clouds in the west over the high horizon of the sea. The sea wind blew, bowing short grasses. A goat bleated in the pastures behind the low, small house. The one window shone dim yellow.

Goha stood her stick and Therru's against the wall by the door, and held the child's hand, and knocked once.

There was no answer.

She pushed the door open. The fire on the hearth was out, cinders and grey ashes, but an oil lamp on the table made a tiny seed of light, and from his mattress on the floor in the far corner of the room Ogion said, "Come in, Tenar."

OGION

SHE BEDDED DOWN THE CHILD ON THE cot in the western alcove. She built up the fire. She went and sat down beside Ogion's pallet, cross-legged on the floor.

"No one looking after you!"

"I sent 'em off," he whispered.

His face was as dark and hard as ever, but his hair was thin and white, and the dim lamp made no spark of light in his eyes.

"You could have died alone," she said, fierce.

"Help me do that," the old man said.

"Not yet," she pleaded, stooping, laying her forehead on his hand.

"Not tonight," he agreed. "Tomorrow."

He lifted his hand to stroke her hair once, having that much strength.

She sat up again. The fire had caught. Its light played on the walls and low ceiling and sent shadows to thicken in the corners of the long room.

"If Ged would come," the old man murmured.

"Have you sent to him?"

"Lost," Ogion said. "He's lost. A cloud. A mist over the lands. He went into the west. Carrying the branch of the rowan tree. Into the dark mist. I've lost my hawk."

"No, no, no," she whispered. "He'll come back."

They were silent. The fire's warmth began to penetrate them both, letting Ogion relax and drift in and out of sleep, letting Tenar find rest pleasant after the long day afoot. She rubbed her feet and her aching shoulders. She had carried Therru part of the last long climb, for the child had begun to gasp with weariness as she tried to keep up.

Tenar got up, heated water, and washed the dust of the road from her. She heated milk, and ate bread she found in Ogion's larder, and came back to sit by him. While he slept, she sat thinking, watching his face and the firelight and the shadows.

She thought how a girl had sat silent, thinking, in the night, a long time ago and far away, a girl in a windowless room, brought up to know herself only as the one who had been eaten, priestess and servant of the powers of the darkness of the earth. And there had been a woman who would sit up in the peaceful silence of a farmhouse when husband and children slept, to think, to be alone an hour. And there was the widow who had carried a burned child here, who sat by the side of the dying, who waited for a man to return. Like all women, any woman, doing what women do. But it was not by the names of the servant or the wife or the widow that Ogion had called her. Nor had Ged, in the darkness of the Tombs. Nor—longer ago, farther away than all—had her mother, the mother she remembered only as the warmth and lion-color of firelight, the mother who had given her her name.

"I am Tenar," she whispered. The fire, catching a dry branch of pine, leaped up in a bright yellow tongue of flame.

Ogion's breathing became troubled and he struggled for air. She helped him as she could till he found some ease. They both slept for a while, she drowsing by his dazed and drifting silence, broken by strange words. Once in the deep night he said aloud, as if meeting a friend in the road, "Are you here, then? Have you seen him?" And again, when Tenar roused herself to build up the fire, he began to speak, but this time it seemed he spoke to someone in his memory of years long gone, for he said clearly as a child might, "I tried to help her, but the roof of the house fell down. It fell on them. It was the earthquake." Tenar listened. She too had seen earthquake. "I tried to help!" said the boy in the old man's voice, in pain. Then the gasping struggle to breathe began again.

At first light Tenar was wakened by a sound she thought at first was the sea. It was a great rushing of wings. A flock of birds was flying over, low, so many that their wings stormed and the window was darkened by their quick shadows. It seemed they circled the house once and then were gone. They made no call or cry, and she did not know what birds they were.

People came that morning from the village of Re Albi, which Ogion's house stood apart from to the north. A goat-girl came, and a woman for the milk of Ogion's goats, and others to ask what they might do for him. Moss, the village witch, fingered the alder stick and the hazel switch by the door and peered in hopefully, but not even she ventured to come in, and Ogion growled from his pallet, "Send 'em away! Send 'em all away!"

He seemed stronger and more comfortable. When little Therru woke, he spoke to her in the dry, kind, quiet way Tenar remembered. The child went out to play in the sun, and he said to Tenar, "What is the name you call her?"

He knew the True Language of the Making, but he had never learned any Kargish at all.

"*Therru* means burning, the flaming of fire," she said.

"Ah, ah," he said, and his eyes gleamed, and he frowned. He seemed to grope for words for a moment. "That one," he said, "that one—they will fear her."

"They fear her now," Tenar said bitterly.

The mage shook his head.

"Teach her, Tenar," he whispered. "Teach her all!—Not Roke. They are afraid—Why did I let you go? Why did you go? To bring her here—too late?"

"Be still, be still," she told him tenderly, for he struggled with words and breath and could find neither. He shook his head, and gasped, "Teach her!" and lay still.

He would not eat, and only drank a little water. In the middle of the day he slept. Waking in the late afternoon, he said, "Now, daughter," and sat up.

Tenar took his hand, smiling at him.

"Help me get up."

"No, no."

"Yes," he said. "Outside. I can't die indoors."

"Where would you go?"

"Anywhere. But if I could, the forest path," he said. "The beech above the meadow."

When she saw he was able to get up and determined to get outdoors, she helped him. Together they got to the door, where he stopped and looked around the one room of his house. In the dark corner to the right of the doorway his tall staff leaned against the wall, shining a little. Tenar reached out to give it to him, but he shook his head. "No," he said, "not that." He looked around again as if for something missing, forgotten. "Come on," he said at last.

When the bright wind from the west blew on his face and he looked out at the high horizon, he said, "That's good."

"Let me get some people from the village to make a litter and carry you," she said. "They're all waiting to do something for you."

"I want to walk," the old man said.

Therru came around the house and watched solemnly as Ogion and Tenar went, step by step, and stopping every five or six steps for Ogion to gasp, across the tangled meadow towards the woods that climbed steep up the mountainside from the inner side of the cliff-top. The sun was hot and the wind cold. It took them a very long time to cross that meadow. Ogion's face was grey and his legs shook like the grass in the wind when they got at last to the foot of a big young beech tree just inside the forest, a few yards up the beginning of the mountain path. There he sank down between the roots of the tree, his back against its trunk. For a long time he could not move or speak, and his heart, pounding and faltering, shook his body. He nodded finally and whispered, "All right."

Therru had followed them at a distance. Tenar went to her and held her and talked to her a little. She came back to Ogion. "She's bringing a rug," she said.

"Not cold."

"*I'm* cold."

There was the flicker of a smile on her face.

The child came lugging a goat's-wool blanket. She whispered to Tenar and ran off again.

"Heather will let her help milk the goats, and

look after her," Tenar said to Ogion. "So I can stay here with you."

"Never one thing, for you," he said in the hoarse whistling whisper that was all the voice he had left.

"No. Always at least two things, and usually more," she said. "But I am here."

He nodded.

For a long time he did not speak, but sat back against the tree trunk, his eyes closed. Watching his face, Tenar saw it change as slowly as the light changed in the west.

He opened his eyes and gazed through a gap in the thickets at the western sky. He seemed to watch something, some act or deed, in that far, clear, golden space of light. He whispered once, hesitant, as if unsure, "The dragon—"

The sun was down, the wind fallen.

Ogion looked at Tenar.

"Over," he whispered with exultation. "All changed!—Changed, Tenar! Wait—wait here, for—" A shaking took his body, tossing him like the branch of a tree in a great wind. He gasped. His eyes closed and opened, gazing beyond her. He laid his hand on hers; she bent down to him; he spoke his name to her, so that after his death he might be truly known.

He gripped her hand and shut his eyes and began once more the struggle to breathe, until there was no more breath. He lay then like one of the roots of the tree, while the stars came out and shone through the leaves and branches of the forest.

Tenar sat with the dead man in the dusk and dark. A lantern gleamed like a firefly across the meadow. She had laid the woolen blanket across them both, but her hand that held his hand had grown cold, as if it held a stone. She touched her forehead to his hand once more. She stood up, stiff and dizzy, her body feeling strange to her, and went to meet and guide whoever was coming with the light.

That night his neighbors sat with Ogion, and he did not send them away.

The mansion house of the Lord of Re Albi stood on an outcrop of rocks on the mountainside above the Overfell. Early in the morning, long before the sun had cleared the mountain, the wizard in the service of that lord came down through the village; and very soon after, another wizard came toiling up the steep road from Gont Port, having set out in darkness. Word had come to them that Ogion was dying, or their power was such that they knew of the passing of a great mage.

The village of Re Albi had no sorcerer, only its mage, and a witchwoman to perform the lowly jobs of finding and mending and bonesetting, which people would not bother the mage with. Aunty Moss was a dour creature, unmarried, like most witches, and unwashed, with greying hair tied in curious charm-knots, and eyes red-rimmed from herbsmoke. It was she who had come across the meadow with the lantern, and with Tenar and the others she had watched the night by Ogion's body. She had set a wax candle in a glass shade, there in the forest, and had burned sweet oils in a dish of clay; she had said the words that should be said, and done what should be done. When it came to touching the body to prepare it for burial, she had looked once at Tenar as if for permission, and then had gone on with her offices. Village witches usually saw to the homing, as they called it, of the dead, and often to the burial.

When the wizard came down from the mansion house, a tall young man with a silvery staff of pinewood, and the other one came up from Gont Port, a stout middle-aged man with a short yew staff, Aunty Moss did not look at them with her bloodshot eyes, but ducked and bowed and drew back, gathering up her poor charms and witcheries.

When she had laid out the corpse as it should lie to be buried, on the left side with the knees bent, she had put in the upturned left hand a tiny charm-bundle, something wrapped in soft goatskin and tied with colored cord. The wizard of Re Albi flicked it away with the tip of his staff.

"Is the grave dug?" asked the wizard of Gont Port.

"Yes," said the wizard of Re Albi. "It is dug in the graveyard of my lord's house," and he pointed towards the mansion house up on the mountain.

"I see," said Gont Port. "I had thought our mage

would be buried in all honor in the city he saved from earthquake."

"My lord desires the honor," said Re Albi.

"But it would seem—" Gont Port began, and stopped, not liking to argue, but not ready to give in to the young man's easy claim. He looked down at the dead man. "He must be buried nameless," he said with regret and bitterness. "I walked all night, but came too late. A great loss made greater!"

The young wizard said nothing.

"His name was Aihal," Tenar said. "His wish was to lie here, where he lies now."

Both men looked at her. The young man, seeing a middle-aged village woman, simply turned away. The man from Gont Port stared a moment and said, "Who are you?"

"I'm called Flint's widow, Goha," she said. "Who I am is your business to know, I think. But not mine to say."

At this, the wizard of Re Albi found her worthy of a brief stare. "Take care, woman, how you speak to men of power!"

"Wait, wait," said Gont Port, with a patting gesture, trying to calm Re Albi's indignation, and still gazing at Tenar. "You were—You were his ward, once?"

"And friend," Tenar said. Then she turned away her head and stood silent. She had heard the anger in her voice as she said that word, "friend." She looked down at her friend, a corpse ready for the ground, lost and still. They stood over him, alive and full of power, offering no friendship, only contempt, rivalry, anger.

"I'm sorry," she said. "It was a long night. I was with him when he died."

"It is not—" the young wizard began, but unexpectedly old Aunty Moss interrupted him, saying loudly, "She was. Yes, she was. Nobody else but her. He sent for her. He sent young Townsend the sheep-dealer to tell her come, clear down round the mountain, and he waited his dying till she did come and was with him, and then he died, and he died where he would be buried, here."

"And," said the older man, "—and he told you—?"

"His name." Tenar looked at them, and do what she would, the incredulity on the older man's face, the contempt on the other's, brought out an answering disrespect in her. "I said that name," she said. "Must I repeat it to you?"

To her consternation she saw from their expressions that in fact they had not heard the name, Ogion's true name; they had not paid attention to her.

"Oh!" she said. "This is a bad time—a time when even such a name can go unheard, can fall like a stone! Is listening not power? Listen, then: his name was Aihal. His name in death is Aihal. In the songs he will be known as Aihal of Gont. If there are songs to be made any more. He was a silent man. Now he's very silent. Maybe there will be no songs, only silence. I don't know. I'm very tired. I've lost my father and dear friend." Her voice failed; her throat closed on a sob. She turned to go. She saw on the forest path the little charm-bundle Aunty Moss had made. She picked it up, knelt down by the corpse, kissed the open palm of the left hand, and laid the bundle on it. There on her knees she looked up once more at the two men. She spoke quietly.

"Will you see to it," she said, "that his grave is dug here, where he desired it?"

First the older man, then the younger, nodded.

She got up, smoothing down her skirt, and started back across the meadow in the morning light.

KALESSIN

"WAIT," OGION, WHO WAS AIHAL NOW, had said to her, just before the wind of death had shaken him and torn him loose from living. "Over—all changed," he had whispered, and then, "Tenar, wait—" But he had not said what she should wait for. The change he had seen or known, perhaps; but what change? Was it his own death he meant, his own life that was over? He had spoken with joy, exulting. He had charged her to wait.

"What else have I to do?" she said to herself, sweeping the floor of his house. "What else have I ever done?" And, speaking to her memory of him, "Shall I wait here, in your house?"

"Yes," said Aihal the Silent, silently, smiling.

So she swept out the house and cleaned the hearth and aired the mattresses. She threw out some chipped crockery and a leaky pan, but she handled them gently. She even put her cheek against a cracked plate as she took it out to the midden, for it was evidence of the old mage's illness this past year. Austere he had been, living as plain as a poor farmer, but when his eyes were clear and his strength in him, he would never have used a broken plate or let a pan go unmended. These signs of his weakness grieved her, making her wish she had been with him to look after him. "I would have liked that," she said to her memory of him, but he said nothing. He never would have anybody to look after him but himself. Would he have said to her, "You have better things to do?" She did not know. He was silent. But that she did right to stay here in his house, now, she was certain.

Shandy and her old husband, Clearbrook, who had been at the farm in Middle Valley longer than she herself had, would look after the flocks and the orchard; the other couple on the farm, Tiff and Sis, would get the field crops in. The rest would have to take care of itself for a while. Her raspberry canes would be picked by the neighborhood children. That was too bad; she loved raspberries. Up here on the Overfell, with the sea wind always blowing, it was too cold to grow raspberries. But Ogion's little old peach tree in the sheltered nook of the house wall facing south bore eighteen peaches, and Therru watched them like a mousing cat till the day she came in and said in her hoarse, unclear voice, "Two of the peaches are all red and yellow."

"Ah," said Tenar. They went together to the peach tree and picked the two first ripe peaches and ate them there, unpeeled. The juice ran down their chins. They licked their fingers.

"Can I plant it?" said Therru, looking at the wrinkled stone of her peach.

"Yes. This is a good place, near the old tree. But not too close. So they both have room for their roots and branches."

The child chose a place and dug the tiny grave. She laid the stone in it and covered it over. Tenar watched her. In the few days they had been living here, Therru had changed, she thought. She was still unresponsive, without anger, without joy; but since they had been here her awful vigilance, her immobility, had almost imperceptibly relaxed. She had desired the peaches. She had thought of planting the stone, of increasing the number of peaches in the world. At Oak Farm she was unafraid of two people only, Tenar and Lark; but here she had taken quite easily to Heather, the goatherd of Re Albi, a bawling-voiced, gentle lackwit of twenty, who treated the child very much as another goat, a lame kid. That was all right. And Aunty Moss was all right too, no matter what she smelled like.

When Tenar had first lived in Re Albi, twenty-five years ago, Moss had not been an old witch but a young one. She had ducked and bowed and grinned at "the young lady," "the White Lady,"

Ogion's ward and student, never speaking to her but with the utmost respect. Tenar had felt that respect to be false, a mask for an envy and dislike and distrust that were all too familiar to her from women over whom she had been placed in a position of superiority, women who saw themselves as common and her as uncommon, as privileged. Priestess of the Tombs of Atuan or foreign ward of the Mage of Gont, she was set apart, set above. Men had given her power, men had shared their power with her. Women looked at her from outside, sometimes rivalrous, often with a trace of ridicule.

She had felt herself the one left outside, shut out. She had fled from the Powers of the desert tombs, and then she had left the powers of learning and skill offered her by her guardian, Ogion. She had turned her back on all that, gone to the other side, the other room, where the women lived, to be one of them. A wife, a farmer's wife, a mother, a householder, undertaking the power that a woman was born to, the authority allotted her by the arrangements of mankind.

And there in the Middle Valley, Flint's wife, Goha, had been welcome, all in all, among the women; a foreigner to be sure, white-skinned and talking a bit strange, but a notable housekeeper, an excellent spinner, with well-behaved, well-grown children and a prospering farm: respectable. And among men she was Flint's woman, doing what a woman should do: bed, breed, bake, cook, clean, spin, sew, serve. A good woman. They approved of her. Flint did well for himself after all, they said. I wonder what a white woman's like, white all over? their eyes said, looking at her, until she got older and they no longer saw her.

Here, now, it was all changed, there was none of all that. Since she and Moss had kept the vigil for Ogion together, the witch had made it plain that she would be her friend, follower, servant, whatever Tenar wanted her to be. Tenar was not at all sure what she wanted Aunty Moss to be, finding her unpredictable, unreliable, incomprehensible, passionate, ignorant, sly, and dirty. But Moss got on with the burned child. Perhaps it was Moss who was working this change, this slight easing, in Therru. With her, Therru behaved as with everyone—blank, unanswering, docile in the way an inanimate thing, a stone, is docile. But the old woman had kept at her, offering her little sweets and treasures, bribing, coaxing, wheedling. "Come with Aunty Moss now, dearie! Come along and Aunty Moss'll show you the prettiest sight you ever saw. . . ."

Moss's nose leaned out over her toothless jaws and thin lips; there was a wart on her cheek the size of a cherry pit; her hair was a grey-black tangle of charm-knots and wisps; and she had a smell as strong and broad and deep and complicated as the smell of a fox's den. "Come into the forest with me, dearie!" said the old witches in the tales told to the children of Gont. "Come with me and I'll show you such a pretty sight!" And then the witch shut the child in her oven and baked it brown and ate it, or dropped it into her well, where it hopped and croaked dismally forever, or put it to sleep for a hundred years inside a great stone, till the King's Son should come, the Mage Prince, to shatter the stone with a word, wake the maiden with a kiss, and slay the wicked witch. . . .

"Come with me, dearie!" And she took the child into the fields and showed her a lark's nest in the green hay, or into the marshes to gather white hallows, wild mint, and blueberries. She did not have to shut the child in an oven, or change her into a monster, or seal her in stone. That had all been done already.

She was kind to Therru, but it was a wheedling kindness, and when they were together it seemed that she talked to the child a great deal. Tenar did not know what Moss was telling or teaching her, whether she should let the witch fill the child's head with stuff. *Weak as woman's magic, wicked as woman's magic*, she had heard said a hundred times. And indeed she had seen that the witchery of such women as Moss or Ivy was often weak in sense and sometimes wicked in intent or through ignorance. Village witches, though they might know many spells and charms and some of the great songs, were never trained in the High Arts or the principles of magery. No woman was so trained. Wizardry was a man's work, a man's skill; magic was made by men. There had never been a woman mage. Though some few had called themselves wizard or sorceress, their power had been untrained, strength without art or knowledge, half frivolous, half dangerous.

The ordinary village witch, like Moss, lived on a few words of the True Speech handed down as great treasures from older witches or bought at high cost from sorcerers, and a supply of common spells of finding and mending, much meaningless ritual and mystery-making and jibberish, a solid experiential training in midwifery, bonesetting, and curing animal and human ailments, a good knowledge of herbs mixed with a mess of superstitions—all this built up on whatever native gift she might have of healing, chanting, changing, or spellcasting. Such a mixture might be a good one or a bad one. Some witches were fierce, bitter women, ready to do harm and knowing no reason not to do harm. Most were midwives and healers with a few love potions, fertility charms, and potency spells on the side, and a good deal of quiet cynicism about them. A few, having wisdom though no learning, used their gift purely for good, though they could not tell, as any prentice wizard could, the reason for what they did, and prate of the Balance and the Way of Power to justify their action or abstention. "I follow my heart," one of these women had said to Tenar when she was Ogion's ward and pupil. "Lord Ogion is a great mage. He does you great honor, teaching you. But look and see, child, if all he's taught you isn't finally to follow your heart."

Tenar had thought even then that the wise woman was right, and yet not altogether right; there was something left out of that. And she still thought so.

Watching Moss with Therru now, she thought Moss was following her heart, but it was a dark, wild, queer heart, like a crow, going its own ways on its own errands. And she thought that Moss might be drawn to Therru not only by kindness but by Therru's hurt, by the harm that had been done her: by violence, by fire.

Nothing Therru did or said, however, showed that she was learning anything from Aunty Moss except where the lark nested and the blueberries grew and how to make cat's cradles one-handed. Therru's right hand had been so eaten by fire that it had healed into a kind of club, the thumb usable only as a pincer, like a crab's claw. But Aunty Moss had an amazing set of cat's cradles for four fingers and a thumb, and rhymes to go with the figures—

> *Churn churn cherry all!*
> *Burn burn bury all!*
> *Come, dragon, come!*

—and the string would form four triangles that flicked into a square. . . . Therru never sang aloud, but Tenar heard her whispering the chant under her breath as she made the figures, alone, sitting on the doorstep of the mage's house.

And, Tenar thought, what bond linked her, herself, to the child, beyond pity, beyond mere duty to the helpless? Lark would have kept her if Tenar had not taken her. But Tenar had taken her without ever asking herself why. Had she been following her heart? Ogion had asked nothing about the child, but he had said, "They will fear her." And Tenar had replied, "They do," and truly. Maybe she herself feared the child, as she feared cruelty, and rape, and fire. Was fear the bond that held her?

"Goha," Therru said, sitting on her heels under the peach tree, looking at the place in the hard summer dirt where she had planted the peach stone, "what are dragons?"

"Great creatures," Tenar said, "like lizards, but longer than a ship—bigger than a house. With wings, like birds. They breathe out fire."

"Do they come here?"

"No," Tenar said.

Therru asked no more.

"Has Aunty Moss been telling you about dragons?"

Therru shook her head. "You did," she said.

"Ah," said Tenar. And presently, "The peach you planted will need water to grow. Once a day, till the rains come."

Therru got up and trotted off around the corner

of the house to the well. Her legs and feet were perfect, unhurt. Tenar liked to see her walk or run, the dark, dusty, pretty little feet on the earth. She came back with Ogion's watering-jug, struggling along with it, and tipped out a small flood over the new planting.

"So you remember the story about when people and dragons were all the same. . . . It told how the humans came here, eastward, but the dragons all stayed in the far western isles. A long, long way away."

Therru nodded. She did not seem to be paying attention, but when Tenar, saying "the western isles," pointed out to the sea, Therru turned her face to the high, bright horizon glimpsed between staked bean-plants and the milking shed.

A goat appeared on the roof of the milking shed and arranged itself in profile to them, its head nobly poised; apparently it considered itself to be a mountain goat.

"Sippy's got loose again," said Tenar.

"Hesssss! Hesssss!" went Therru, imitating Heather's goat call; and Heather herself appeared by the bean-patch fence, saying "Hesssss!" up at the goat, which ignored her, gazing thoughtfully down at the beans.

Tenar left the three of them to play the catching-Sippy game. She wandered on past the bean patch towards the edge of the cliff and along it. Ogion's house stood apart from the village and closer than any other house to the edge of the Overfell, here a steep, grassy slope broken by ledges and outcrops of rock, where goats could be pastured. As you went on north the drop grew ever steeper, till it began to fall sheer; and on the path the rock of the great ledge showed through the soil, till a mile or so north of the village the Overfell had narrowed to a shelf of reddish sandstone hanging above the sea that undercut its base two thousand feet below.

Nothing grew at that far end of the Overfell but lichens and rockworts and here and there a blue daisy, wind-stunted, like a button dropped on the rough, crumbling stone. Inland of the cliff's edge to the north and east, above a narrow strip of marshland the dark, tremendous side of Gont Mountain rose up, forested almost to the peak. The cliff stood so high above the bay that one must look down to see its outer shores and the vague lowlands of Essary. Beyond them, in all the south and west, there was nothing but the sky above the sea.

Tenar had liked to go there in the years she had lived in Re Albi. Ogion had loved the forests, but she, who had lived in a desert where the only trees for a hundred miles were a gnarled orchard of peach and apple, hand watered in the endless summers, where nothing grew green and moist and easy, where there was nothing but a mountain and a great plain and the sky—she liked the cliff's edge better than the enclosing woods. She liked having nothing at all over her head.

The lichens, the grey rockwort, the stemless daisies, she liked them too; they were familiar. She sat down on the shelving rock a few feet from the edge and looked out to sea as she had used to do. The sun was hot but the ceaseless wind cooled the sweat on her face and arms. She leaned back on her hands and thought of nothing, sun and wind and sky and sea filling her, making her transparent to sun, wind, sky, sea. But her left hand reminded her of its existence, and she looked round to see what was scratching the heel of her hand. It was a tiny thistle, crouched in a crack in the sandstone, barely lifting its colorless spikes into the light and wind. It nodded stiffly as the wind blew, resisting the wind, rooted in rock. She gazed at it for a long time.

When she looked out to sea again she saw, blue in the blue haze where sea met sky, the line of an island: Oranéa, easternmost of the Inner Isles.

She gazed at that faint dream-shape, dreaming, until a bird flying from the west over the sea drew her gaze. It was not a gull, for it flew steadily, and too high to be a pelican. Was it a wild goose, or an albatross, the great, rare voyager of the open sea, come among the islands? She watched the slow beat of the wings, far out and high in the dazzling air. Then she got to her feet, retreating a little from the cliff's edge, and stood motionless, her heart going hard and her breath caught in her throat, watching the sinuous, iron-dark body borne by long, webbed wings as red as fire, the outreaching claws, the coils of smoke fading behind it in the air.

Straight to Gont it flew, straight to the Overfell, straight to her. She saw the glitter of rust-black scales and the gleam of the long eye. She saw the red tongue that was a tongue of flame. The stink of burning filled the wind, as with a hissing roar the dragon, turning to land on the shelf of rock, breathed out a sigh of fire.

Its feet clashed on the rock. The thorny tail, writhing, rattled, and the wings, scarlet where the sun shone through them, stormed and rustled as they folded down to the mailed flanks. The head turned slowly. The dragon looked at the woman who stood there within reach of its scythe-blade talons. The woman looked at the dragon. She felt the heat of its body.

She had been told that men must not look into a dragon's eyes, but that was nothing to her. It gazed straight at her from yellow eyes under armored carapaces wide-set above the narrow nose and flaring, fuming nostrils. And her small, soft face and dark eyes gazed straight at it.

Neither of them spoke.

The dragon turned its head aside a little so that she was not destroyed when it did speak, or perhaps it laughed—a great "Hah!" of orange flame.

Then it lowered its body into a crouch and spoke, but not to her.

"*Ahivaraihe, Ged*," it said, mildly enough, smokily,

with a flicker of the burning tongue; and it lowered its head.

Tenar saw for the first time, then, the man astride its back. In the notch between two of the high sword-thorns that rose in a row down its spine he sat, just behind the neck and above the shoulders where the wings had root. His hands were clenched on the rust-dark mail of the dragon's neck and his head leaned against the base of the sword-thorn, as if he were asleep.

"*Ahi eheraihe, Ged!*" said the dragon, a little louder, its long mouth seeming always to smile, showing the teeth as long as Tenar's forearm, yellowish, with white, sharp tips.

The man did not stir.

The dragon turned its long head and looked again at Tenar.

"*Sobriost,*" it said, in a whisper of steel sliding over steel.

That word of the Language of the Making she knew. Ogion had taught her all she would learn of that tongue. Go up, the dragon said: mount! And she saw the steps to mount. The taloned foot, the crooked elbow, the shoulder-joint, the first musculature of the wing: four steps.

She too said, "Hah!" but not in a laugh, only trying to get her breath, which kept sticking in her throat; and she lowered her head a moment to stop her dizzy faintness. Then she went forward, past the talons and the long lipless mouth and the long yellow eye, and mounted the shoulder of the dragon. She took the man's arm. He did not move, but surely he was not dead, for the dragon had brought him here and spoken to him. "Come on," she said, and then seeing his face as she loosened the clenched grip of his left hand, "Come on, Ged. Come on. . . ."

He raised his head a little. His eyes were open, but unseeing. She had to climb around him, scratching her legs on the hot, mailed hide of the dragon, and unclench his right hand from a horny knob at the base of the sword-thorn. She got him to take hold of her arms, and so could carry-drag him down those four strange stairs to earth.

He roused enough to try to hold on to her, but there was no strength in him. He sprawled off the dragon onto the rock like a sack unloaded, and lay there.

The dragon turned its immense head and in a completely animal gesture nosed and sniffed at the man's body.

It lifted its head, and its wings too half lifted with a vast, metallic sound. It shifted its feet away from Ged, closer to the edge of the cliff. Turning back the head on the thorned neck, it stared once more directly at Tenar, and its voice like the dry roar of a kiln-fire spoke: "*Thesse Kalessin*."

The sea wind whistled in the dragon's half-open wings.

"*Thesse Tenar*," the woman said in a clear, shaking voice.

The dragon looked away, westward, over the sea. It twitched its long body with a clink and clash of iron scales, then abruptly opened its wings, crouched, and leapt straight out from the cliff onto the wind. The dragging tail scored the sandstone as it passed. The red wings beat down, lifted, and beat down, and already Kalessin was far from land, flying straight, flying west.

Tenar watched it till it was no larger than a wild goose or a gull. The air was cold. When the dragon had been there it had been hot, furnace-hot, with the dragon's inward fire. Tenar shivered. She sat down on the rock beside Ged and began to cry. She hid her face in her arms and wept aloud. "What can I do?" she cried. "What can I do now?"

Presently she wiped her eyes and nose on her sleeve, put back her hair with both hands, and turned to the man who lay beside her. He lay so still, so easy on the bare rock, as if he might lie there forever.

Tenar sighed. There was nothing she could do, but there was always the next thing to be done.

She could not carry him. She would have to get help. That meant leaving him alone. It seemed to her that he was too near the cliff's edge. If he tried to get up he might fall, weak and dizzy as he would be. How could she move him? He did not rouse at all when she spoke and touched him. She took him under the shoulders and tried to pull him, and to her surprise succeeded; dead weight as he was, the weight was not much. Resolute, she dragged him ten or fifteen feet inland, off the bare rock shelf onto a bit of dirt, where dry bunchgrass gave some illusion of shelter. There she had to leave him. She could not run, for her legs shook and her breath still came in sobs. She walked as fast as she could to Ogion's house, calling out as she approached it to Heather, Moss, and Therru.

The child appeared around the milking shed and stood, as her way was, obedient to Tenar's call but not coming forward to greet or be greeted.

"Therru, run into town and ask anyone to come—anybody strong—There's a man hurt on the cliff."

Therru stood there. She had never gone alone into the village. She was frozen between obedience and fear. Tenar saw that and said, "Is Aunty Moss here? Is Heather? The three of us can carry him. Only, quick, quick, Therru!" She felt that if she let Ged lie unprotected there he would surely die. He would be gone when she came back—dead, fallen, taken by dragons. Anything could happen. She must hurry before it happened. Flint had died of a stroke in his fields and she had not been with him. He had died alone. The shepherd had found him lying by the gate. Ogion had died and she could not keep him from dying, she could not give him breath. Ged had come home to die and it was the end of everything, there was nothing left, nothing to be done, but she must do it. "Quick, Therru! Bring anyone!"

She started shakily towards the village herself, but saw old Moss hurrying across the pasture, stumping along with her thick hawthorn stick. "Did you call me, dearie?"

Moss's presence was an immediate relief. She began to get her breath and be able to think. Moss wasted no time in questions, but hearing there was a man hurt who must be moved, got the heavy canvas mattress-cover that Tenar had been airing, and lugged it out to the end of the Overfell. She and Tenar rolled Ged onto it and were dragging this conveyance laboriously homeward when Heather came trotting along, followed by Therru and Sippy. Heather was young and strong, and with her help they could lift the canvas like a litter and carry the man to the house.

Tenar and Therru slept in the alcove in the west wall of the long single room. There was only Ogion's bed at the far end, covered now with a heavy linen sheet. There they laid the man. Tenar put Ogion's blanket over him, while Moss muttered charms around the bed, and Heather and Therru stood and stared.

"Let him be now," said Tenar, leading them all to the front part of the house.

"Who is he?" Heather asked.

"What was he doing on the Overfell?" Moss asked.

"You know him, Moss. He was Ogion's—Aihal's prentice, once."

The witch shook her head. "That was the lad from Ten Alders, dearie," she said. "The one that's Archmage in Roke, now."

Tenar nodded.

"No, dearie," said Moss. "This looks like him. But isn't him. This man's no mage. Not even a sorcerer."

Heather looked from one to the other, entertained. She did not understand most things people said, but she liked to hear them say them.

"But I know him, Moss. It's Sparrowhawk." Saying the name, Ged's use-name, released a tenderness in her, so that for the first time she thought and felt that this was he indeed, and that all the years since she had first seen him were their bond. She saw a light like a star in darkness, underground, long ago, and his face in the light. "I know him, Moss." She smiled, and then smiled more broadly. "He's the first man I ever saw," she said.

Moss mumbled and shifted. She did not like to contradict "Mistress Goha," but she was perfectly unconvinced. "There's tricks, disguises, transformations, changes," she said. "Better be careful, dearie. How did he get where you found him, away out there? Did any see him come through the village?"

"None of you—saw—?"

They stared at her. She tried to say "the dragon" and could not. Her lips and tongue would not form the word. But a word formed itself with them, making itself with her mouth and breath. "Kalessin," she said.

Therru was staring at her. A wave of warmth, heat, seemed to flow from the child, as if she were in fever. She said nothing, but moved her lips as if repeating the name, and that fever heat burned around her.

"Tricks!" Moss said. "Now that our mage is gone there'll be all kinds of tricksters coming round."

"I came from Atuan to Havnor, from Havnor to Gont, with Sparrowhawk, in an open boat," Tenar said drily. "You saw him when he brought me here, Moss. He wasn't archmage then. But he was the same, the same man. Are there other scars like those?"

Confronted, the older woman became still, collecting herself. She glanced at Therru. "No," she said. "But—"

"Do you think I wouldn't know him?"

Moss twisted her mouth, frowned, rubbed one thumb with the other, looking at her hands. "There's evil things in the world, mistress," she said. "A thing that takes a man's form and body, but his soul's gone—eaten—"

"The gebbeth?"

Moss cringed at the word spoken openly. She nodded. "They do say, once the mage Sparrowhawk came here, long ago, before you came with him. And a thing of darkness came with him—following him. Maybe it still does. Maybe—"

"The dragon who brought him here," Tenar said, "called him by his true name. And I know that name." Wrath at the witch's obstinate suspicion rang in her voice.

Moss stood mute. Her silence was better argument than her words.

"Maybe the shadow on him is his death," Tenar said. "Maybe he's dying. I don't know. If Ogion—"

At the thought of Ogion she was in tears again, thinking how Ged had come too late. She swallowed the tears and went to the woodbox for kindling for the fire. She gave Therru the kettle to fill, touching her face as she spoke to her. The seamed and slabby scars were hot to touch, but the child was not feverish. Tenar knelt to make the fire. Somebody in this fine household—a witch, a widow, a cripple, and a half-wit—had to do what must be done, and not frighten the child with weeping. But the dragon was gone, and was there nothing to come any more but death?

Bettering

HE LAY LIKE THE DEAD BUT WAS NOT DEAD. Where had he been? What had he come through? That night, in firelight, Tenar took the stained, worn, sweat-stiffened clothes off him. She washed him and let him lie naked between the linen sheet and the blanket of soft, heavy goat's-wool. Though a short, slight-built man, he had been compact, vigorous; now he was thin as if worn down to the bone, worn away, fragile. Even the scars that ridged his shoulder and the left side of his face from temple to jaw seemed lessened, silvery. And his hair was grey.

I'm sick of mourning, Tenar thought. Sick of mourning, sick of grief. I will not grieve for him! Didn't he come to me riding the dragon?

Once I meant to kill him, she thought. Now I'll

make him live, if I can. She looked at him then with a challenge in her eye, and no pity.

"Which of us saved the other from the Labyrinth, Ged?"

Unhearing, unmoving, he slept. She was very tired. She bathed in the water she had heated to wash him with, and crept into bed beside the little, warm, silky silence that was Therru asleep. She slept, and her sleep opened out into a vast windy space hazy with rose and gold. She flew. Her voice called, "Kalessin!" A voice answered, calling from the gulfs of light.

When she woke, the birds were chirping in the fields and on the roof. Sitting up she saw the light of morning through the gnarled glass of the low window looking west. There was something in her, some seed or glimmer, too small to look at or think about, new. Therru was still asleep. Tenar sat by her looking out the small window at cloud and sunlight, thinking of her daughter Apple, trying to remember Apple as a baby. Only the faintest glimpse, vanishing as she turned to it—the small, fat body shaking with a laugh, the wispy, flying hair. . . . And the second baby, Spark he got called as a joke, because he'd been struck off Flint. She did not know his true name. He had been as sickly a child as Apple had been a sound one. Born early and very small, he had nearly died of the croup at two months, and for two years after that it had been like rearing a fledgling sparrow, you never knew if he would be alive in the morning. But he held on, the little spark wouldn't go out. And growing, he became a wiry boy, endlessly active, driven; no use on the farm; no patience with animals, plants, people; using words for his needs only, never for pleasure and the give and take of love and knowledge.

Ogion had come by on his wanderings when Apple was thirteen and Spark eleven. Ogion had named Apple then, in the springs of the Kaheda at the valley's head; beautiful she had walked in the green water, the woman-child, and he had given her her true name, Hayohe. He had stayed on at Oak Farm a day or two, and had asked the boy if he wanted to go wandering a little with him in the forests. Spark merely shook his head. "What would you do if you could?" the mage had asked him, and the boy said what he had never been able to say to father or mother: "Go to sea." So after Beech gave him his true name, three years later, he shipped as a sailor aboard a merchantman trading from Valmouth to Oranéa and North Havnor. From time to time he would come to the farm, but not often and never for long, though at his father's death it would be his property. He was white-skinned like Tenar, but grew tall like Flint, with a narrow face. He had not told his parents his true name. There might never be anyone he told it to. Tenar had not seen him for three years now. He might or might not know of his father's death. He might be dead himself, drowned, but she thought not. He would carry that spark his life over the waters, through the storms.

That was what it was like in her now, a spark; like the bodily certainty of a conception; a change, a new thing. What it was she would not ask. You did not ask. You did not ask a true name. It was given you, or not.

She got up and dressed. Early as it was, it was warm, and she built no fire. She sat in the doorway to drink a cup of milk and watch the shadow of Gont Mountain draw inward from the sea. There was as little wind as there could be on this air-swept shelf of rock, and the breeze had a midsummer feel, soft and rich, smelling of the meadows. There was a sweetness in the air, a change.

"All changed!" the old man had whispered, dying, joyful. Laying his hand on hers, giving her the gift, his name, giving it away.

"Aihal!" she whispered. For answer a couple of goats bleated, out behind the milking shed, waiting for Heather to come. "Be-eh," one said, and the other, deeper, metallic, "Bla-ah! Bla-ah!" Trust a goat, Flint used to say, to spoil anything. Flint, a shepherd, had disliked goats. But Sparrowhawk had been a goatherd, here across the mountain, as a boy.

She went inside. She found Therru standing gazing at the sleeping man. She put her arm around the child, and though Therru usually shrank from or was passive to touch or caress, this time she accepted it and perhaps even leaned a little to Tenar.

Ged lay in the same exhausted, overwhelmed sleep. His face was turned to expose the four white scars that marked it.

"Was he burned?" Therru whispered.

Tenar did not answer at once. She did not know what those scars were. She had asked him long ago, in the Painted Room of the Labyrinth of Atuan, jeering: "A dragon?" And he had answered seriously, "Not a dragon. One of the kinship of the Nameless Ones; but I learned his name. . . ." And that was all she knew. But she knew what "burned" meant to the child.

"Yes," she said.

Therru continued to gaze at him. She had cocked her head to bring her one seeing eye to bear, which made her look like a little bird, a sparrow or a finch.

"Come along, finchling, birdlet, sleep's what he needs, you need a peach. Is there a peach ripe this morning?"

Therru trotted out to see, and Tenar followed her.

Eating her peach, the child studied the place where she had planted the peach pit yesterday. She was evidently disappointed that no tree had grown there, but she said nothing.

"Water it," said Tenar.

Aunty Moss arrived in the midmorning. One of her skills as a witch-handywoman was basket making, using the rushes of Overfell Marsh, and Tenar had asked her to teach her the art. As a child in Atuan, Tenar had learned how to learn. As a stranger in Gont, she had found that people liked to teach. She had learned to be taught and so to be accepted, her foreignness forgiven.

Ogion had taught her his knowledge, and then Flint had taught her his. It was her habit of life, to learn. There seemed always to be a great deal to be learned, more than she would have believed when she was a prentice-priestess or the pupil of a mage.

The rushes had been soaking, and this morning they were to split them, an exacting but not a complicated business, leaving plenty of attention to spare.

"Aunty," said Tenar as they sat on the doorstep with the bowl of soaking rushes between them and a mat before them to lay the split ones on, "how do you tell if a man's a wizard or not?"

Moss's reply was circuitous, beginning with the usual gnomics and obscurities. "Deep knows deep," she said, deeply, and "What's born will speak," and she told a story about the ant that picked up a tiny end of hair from the floor of a palace and ran off to the ants' nest with it, and in the night the nest glowed underground like a star, for the hair was from the head of the great mage Brost. But only the wise could see the glowing anthill. To common eyes it was all dark.

"One needs training, then," said Tenar.

Maybe, maybe not, was the gist of Moss's dark

reply. "Some are born with that gift," she said. "Even when they don't know it, it will be there. Like the hair of the mage in the hole in the ground, it will shine."

"Yes," said Tenar. "I've seen that." She split and resplit a reed cleanly and laid the splints on the mat. "How do you know, then, when a man is *not* a wizard?"

"It's not there," Moss said, "it's not there, dearie. The power. See now. If I've got eyes in my head I can see that you have eyes, can't I? And if you're blind I'll see that. And if you've only got one eye, like the little one, or if you've got three, I'll see 'em, won't I? But if I don't have an eye to see with, I won't know if you do till you tell me. But I do. I see, I know. The third eye!" She touched her forehead and gave a loud, dry chuckle, like a hen triumphant over an egg. She was pleased with having found the words to say what she wanted to say. A good deal of her obscurity and cant, Tenar had begun to realize, was mere ineptness with words and ideas. Nobody had ever taught her to think consecutively. Nobody had ever listened to what she said. All that was expected, all that was wanted of her was muddle, mystery, mumbling. She was a witchwoman. She had nothing to do with clear meaning.

"I understand," Tenar said. "Then—maybe this is a question you don't want to answer—then when you look at a person with your third eye, with your power, you see their power—or don't see it?"

"It's more a knowing," Moss said. "Seeing is just a way of saying it. 'Tisn't like I see you, I see this rush, I see the mountain there. It's a knowing. I know what's in you and not in that poor hollow-headed Heather. I know what's in the dear child and not in him in yonder. I know—" She could not get any farther with it. She mumbled and spat. "Any witch worth a hairpin knows another witch!" she said finally, plainly, impatiently.

"You recognize each other."

Moss nodded. "Aye, that's it. That's the word. Recognize."

"And a wizard would recognize your power, would know you for a sorceress—"

But Moss was grinning at her, a black cave of a grin in a cobweb of wrinkles.

"Dearie," she said, "a man, you mean, a wizardly man? What's a man of power to do with us?"

"But Ogion—"

"Lord Ogion was kind," Moss said, without irony.

They split rushes for a while in silence.

"Don't cut your thumb on 'em, dearie," Moss said.

"Ogion taught me. As if I weren't a girl. As if I'd been his prentice, like Sparrowhawk. He taught me the Language of the Making, Moss. What I asked him, he told me."

"There wasn't no other like him."

"It was I who wouldn't be taught. I left him. What did I want with his books? What good were they to me? I wanted to live, I wanted a man, I wanted my children, I wanted my life."

She split reeds neatly, quickly, with her nail.

"And I got it," she said.

"Take with the right hand, throw away with the left," the witch said. "Well, dearie mistress, who's to say? Who's to say? Wanting a man got me into awful troubles more than once. But wanting to get married, never! No, no. None of that for me."

"Why not?" Tenar demanded.

Taken aback, Moss said simply, "Why, what man'd marry a witch?" And then, with a sidelong chewing motion of her jaw, like a sheep shifting its cud, "And what witch'd marry a man?"

They split rushes.

"What's wrong with men?" Tenar inquired cautiously.

As cautiously, lowering her voice, Moss replied, "I don't know, my dearie. I've thought on it. Often I've thought on it. The best I can say it is like this. A man's in his skin, see, like a nut in its shell." She held up her long, bent, wet fingers as if holding a walnut. "It's hard and strong, that shell, and it's all full of him. Full of grand man-meat, manself. And that's all. That's all there is. It's all him and nothing else, inside."

Tenar pondered awhile and finally asked, "But if he's a wizard—"

"Then it's all his power, inside. His power's himself, see. That's how it is with him. And that's all. When his power goes, he's gone. Empty." She cracked the unseen walnut and tossed the shells away. "Nothing."

"And a woman, then?"

"Oh, well, dearie, a woman's a different thing entirely. Who knows where a woman begins and ends? Listen, mistress, I have roots, I have roots deeper than this island. Deeper than the sea, older than the raising of the lands. I go back into the dark." Moss's eyes shone with a weird brightness in their red rims and her voice sang like an instrument. "I go back into the dark! Before the moon I was. No one knows, no one knows, no one can say what I am, what a woman is, a woman of power, a woman's power, deeper than the roots of trees, deeper than the roots of islands, older than the Making, older than the moon. Who dares ask questions of the dark? Who'll ask the dark its name?"

The old woman was rocking, chanting, lost in her incantation; but Tenar sat upright, and split a reed down the center with her thumbnail.

"I will," she said.

She split another reed.

"I lived long enough in the dark," she said.

She looked in from time to time to see that Sparrowhawk was still sleeping. She did so now. When she sat down again with Moss, wanting not to return to what they had been saying, for the older woman looked dour and sullen, she said, "This morning when I woke up I felt, oh, as if a new wind were blowing. A change. Maybe just the weather. Did you feel that?"

But Moss would not say yes or no. "Many a wind blows here on the Overfell, some good, some ill. Some bears clouds and some fair weather, and some brings news to those who can hear it, but those who won't listen can't hear. Who am I to know, an old woman without mage-learning, without book-learning? All my learning's in the earth, in the dark earth. Under their feet, the proud ones. Under their feet, the proud lords and mages. Why should they look down, the learned ones? What does an old witch-woman know?"

She would be a formidable enemy, Tenar thought, and was a difficult friend.

"Aunty," she said, taking up a reed, "I grew up among women. Only women. In the Kargish lands, far east, in Atuan. I was taken from my family as a little child to be brought up a priestess in a place in the desert. I don't know what name it has, all we called it in our language was just that, the place. The only place I knew. There were a few soldiers guarding it, but they couldn't come inside the walls. And we couldn't go outside the walls. Only in a group, all women and girls, with eunuchs guarding us, keeping the men out of sight."

"What's those you said?"

"Eunuchs?" Tenar had used the Kargish word without thinking. "Gelded men," she said.

The witch stared, and said, "*Tsekh!*" and made the sign to avert evil. She sucked her lips. She had been startled out of her resentment.

"One of them was the nearest to a mother I had there. . . . But do you see, Aunty, I never saw a man till I was a woman grown. Only girls and women. And yet I didn't know what women are, because women were all I did know. Like men who live among men, sailors, and soldiers, and mages on Roke—do they know what men are? How can they, if they never speak to a woman?"

"Do they take 'em and do 'em like rams and he-goats," said Moss, "like that, with a gelding knife?"

Horror, the macabre, and a gleam of vengeance had won out over both anger and reason. Moss didn't want to pursue any topic but that of eunuchs.

Tenar could not tell her much. She realized that she had never thought about the matter. When she was a girl in Atuan, there had been gelded men; and one of them had loved her tenderly, and she him; and she had killed him to escape from him. Then she had come to the Archipelago, where there were no eunuchs, and had forgotten them, sunk them in darkness with Manan's body.

"I suppose," she said, trying to satisfy Moss's craving for details, "that they took young boys, and—" But she stopped. Her hands stopped working.

"Like Therru," she said after a long pause. "What's a child for? What's it there for? To be used. To be raped, to be gelded— Listen, Moss. When I lived in the dark places, that was what they did there. And when I came here, I thought I'd come out into the light. I learned the true words. And I had my man, I bore my children, I lived well. In the broad daylight. And in the broad daylight, they did that—to the child. In the meadows by the river. The river that rises from the spring where Ogion named my daughter. In the sunlight. I am trying to find out where I can live, Moss. Do you know what I mean? What I'm trying to say?"

"Well, well," the older woman said; and after a while, "Dearie, there's misery enough without going looking for it." And seeing Tenar's hands shake as she tried to split a stubborn reed, she said, again, "Don't cut your thumb on 'em, dearie."

It was not till the next day that Ged roused at all. Moss, who was very skillful though appallingly unclean as a nurse, had succeeded in spooning some meat-broth into him. "Starving," she said, "and dried up with thirst. Wherever he was, they didn't do much eating and drinking." And after appraising him again, "He'll be too far gone already, I think. They get weak, see, and can't even drink, though it's all they need. I've known a great strong man to die like that. All in a few days, shriveled to a shadow, like."

But through relentless patience she got a few spoonfuls of her brew of meat and herbs into him. "Now we'll see," she said. "Too late, I guess. He's slipping away." She spoke without regret, perhaps with relish. The man was nothing to her; a death was an event. Maybe she could bury this mage. They had not let her bury the old one.

Tenar was salving his hands, the next day, when he woke. He must have ridden long on Kalessin's back, for his fierce grip on the iron scales had scoured the skin off his palms, and the inner side of the fingers was cut and recut. Sleeping, he kept his hands clenched as if they would not let go the absent dragon. She had to force his fingers open gently to wash and salve the sores. As she did that, he cried out and started, reaching out, as if he felt himself falling. His eyes opened. She spoke quietly. He looked at her.

"Tenar," he said without smiling, in pure recognition beyond emotion. And it gave her pure pleasure, like a sweet flavor or a flower, that there was still one man living who knew her name, and that it was this man.

She leaned forward and kissed his cheek. "Lie still," she said. "Let me finish this." He obeyed, drifting back into sleep soon, this time with his hands open and relaxed.

Later, falling asleep beside Therru in the night, she thought, But I never kissed him before. And the thought shook her. At first she disbelieved it. Surely, in all the years— Not in the Tombs, but after, traveling together in the mountains— In *Lookfar*, when they sailed together to Havnor— When he brought her here to Gont—?

No. Nor had Ogion ever kissed her, or she him. He had called her daughter, and had loved her, but had not touched her; and she, brought up as a solitary, untouched priestess, a holy thing, had not sought touch, or had not known she sought it. She would lean her forehead or her cheek for a moment on Ogion's open hand, and he might stroke her hair, once, very lightly.

And Ged never even that.

Did I never *think* of it? she asked herself in a kind of incredulous awe.

She did not know. As she tried to think of it, a horror, a sense of transgression, came on her very strongly, and then died away, meaningless. Her lips knew the slightly rough, dry, cool skin of his cheek near the mouth on the right side, and only that knowledge had importance, was of weight.

She slept. She dreamed that a voice called her, "Tenar! Tenar!" and that she replied, crying like a seabird, flying in the light above the sea; but she did not know what name she called.

Sparrowhawk disappointed Aunty Moss. He stayed alive. After a day or two she gave him up for saved. She came and fed him her broth of goat's-meat and roots and herbs, propping him against her, surrounding him with the powerful smell of her body, spooning life into him, and grumbling. Although he had recognized her and called her by her use-name, and she could not deny that he seemed to be the man called Sparrowhawk, she wanted to deny it. She did not like him. He was all wrong, she said. Tenar respected the witch's sagacity enough that this troubled her, but she could not find any such suspicion in herself, only the pleasure of his being there and of his slow return to life. "When he's himself again, you'll see," she said to Moss.

"Himself!" Moss said, and she made that gesture with her fingers of breaking and dropping a nutshell.

He asked, pretty soon, about Ogion. Tenar had dreaded that question. She had told herself and nearly convinced herself that he would not ask, that he would know as mages knew, as even the wizards of Gont Port and Re Albi had known when Ogion died. But on the fourth morning he was lying awake when she came to him, and looking up at her, he said, "This is Ogion's house."

"Aihal's house," she said, as easily as she could; it still was not easy for her to speak the mage's true name. She did not know if Ged had known that name. Surely he had. Ogion would have told him, or had not needed to tell him.

For a while he did not react, and when he spoke it was without expression. "Then he is dead."

"Ten days ago."

He lay looking before him as if pondering, trying to think something out.

"When did I come here?"

She had to lean close to understand him.

"Four days ago, in the evening of the day."

"There was no one else in the mountains," he said. Then his body winced and shuddered as if in pain or the intolerable memory of pain. He shut his eyes, frowning, and took a deep breath.

As his strength returned little by little, that frown, the held breath and clenched hands, became familiar to Tenar. Strength returned to him but not ease, not health.

He sat on the doorstep of the house in the sunlight of the summer afternoon. It was the longest journey he had yet taken from the bed. He sat on the threshold, looking out into the day, and Tenar, coming around the house from the bean patch, looked at him. He still had an ashy, shadowy look to him. It was not the grey hair only, but some quality of skin and bone, and there was nothing much to him but that. There was no light in his eyes. Yet this shadow, this ashen man, was the same whose face she had seen first in the radiance of his own power, the strong face with hawk nose and fine mouth, a handsome man. He had always been a proud, handsome man.

She came on towards him.

"The sunlight's what you need," she said to him, and he nodded, but his hands were clenched as he sat in the flood of summer warmth.

He was so silent with her that she thought maybe it was her presence that troubled him. Maybe he could not be at ease with her as he had used to be. He was Archmage now, after all—she kept forgetting that. And it was twenty-five years since they had walked in the mountains of Atuan and sailed together in *Lookfar* across the eastern sea.

"Where is *Lookfar*?" she asked, suddenly, surprised by the thought of it, and then thought, But how stupid of me! All those years ago, and he's Archmage, he wouldn't have that little boat now.

"In Selidor," he answered, his face set in its steady and incomprehensible misery.

As long ago as forever, as far away as Selidor. . . .

"The farthest island," she said; it was half a question.

"The farthest west," he said.

They were sitting at table, having finished the evening meal. Therru had gone outside to play.

"It was from Selidor that you came, then, on Kalessin?"

When she spoke the dragon's name again it spoke itself, shaping her mouth to its shape and sound, making her breath soft fire.

At the name, he looked up at her, one intense glance, which made her realize that he did not usually meet her eyes at all. He nodded. Then, with a laborious honesty, he corrected his assent: "From Selidor to Roke. And then from Roke to Gont."

A thousand miles? Ten thousand miles? She had no idea. She had seen the great maps in the treasuries of Havnor, but no one had taught her numbers, distances. *As far away as Selidor* . . . And could the flight of a dragon be counted in miles?

"Ged," she said, using his true name since they were alone, "I know you've been in great pain and peril. And if you don't want, maybe you can't, maybe you shouldn't tell me—but if I knew, if I knew something of it, I'd be more help to you, maybe. I'd like to be. And they'll be coming soon from Roke for you, sending a ship for the Archmage, what do I know, sending a dragon for you! And you'll be gone again. And we'll never have talked." As she spoke she clenched her own hands at the falseness of her tone and words. To joke about the dragon—to whine like an accusing wife!

He was looking down at the table, sullen, enduring, like a farmer after a hard day in the fields faced with some domestic squall.

"Nobody will come from Roke, I think," he said, and it cost him effort enough that it was a while before he went on. "Give me time."

She thought it was all he was going to say, and replied, "Yes, of course. I'm sorry," and was rising to clear the table when he said, still looking down, not clearly, "I have that, now."

Then he too got up, and brought his dish to the sink, and finished clearing the table. He washed the dishes while Tenar put the food away. And that interested her. She had been comparing him to Flint; but Flint had never washed a dish in his life. Women's work. But Ged and Ogion had lived here, bachelors, without women; everywhere Ged had lived, it was without women; so he did the "women's work" and thought nothing about it. It would be a pity, she thought, if he did think about it, if he started fearing that his dignity hung by a dishcloth.

Nobody came for him from Roke. When they spoke of it, there had scarcely been time for any ship but one with the magewind in her sails all the way; but the days went on, and still there was no message or sign to him. It seemed strange to her that they would let their archmage go untroubled so long. He must have forbidden them to send to him; or perhaps he had hidden himself here with his wizardry, so that they did not know where he was, and so that he could not be recognized. For the villagers paid curiously little attention to him still.

That no one had come down from the mansion of the Lord of Re Albi was less surprising. The lords of that house had never been on good terms with Ogion. Women of the house had been, so the village tales went, adepts of dark arts. One had married a northern lord, they said, who buried her alive under a stone; another had meddled with the unborn child in her womb, trying to make it a creature of power, and indeed it had spoken words as it was born, but it had no bones. "Like a little bag of skin," the midwife whispered in the village, "a little bag with eyes and a voice, and it never sucked, but it spoke in some strange tongue, and died. . . ." Whatever the truth of such tales, the Lords of Re Albi had always held aloof. Companion of the mage Sparrowhawk, ward of the mage Ogion, bringer of the Ring of Erreth-Akbe to Havnor, Tenar might have been asked to stay, it would seem, at the mansion house when she first came to Re Albi; but she had not. She had lived instead, to her own delight, alone in a tiny cottage that belonged to the village weaver, Fan, and she saw the people of the great house seldom and at a distance. There was now no lady of the house at all, Moss told her, only the old lord, very old, and his grandson, and the young wizard, called Aspen, whom they had hired from the School on Roke.

Since Ogion was buried, with Aunty Moss's talisman in his hand, under the beech tree by the mountain path, Tenar had not seen Aspen. Strange as it seemed, he did not know the Archmage of Earthsea was in his own village, or, if he knew it, for some reason kept away. And the wizard of Gont Port, who had also come to bury Ogion, had never come back either. Even if he did not know that Ged was here, surely he knew who she was, the White Lady, who had worn the Ring of Erreth-Akbe on her wrist, who had made whole the Rune of Peace— And how many years ago was that, old woman! she said to herself. Is your nose out of joint?

All the same, it was she who had told them Ogion's true name. It seemed some courtesy was owing.

But wizards, as such, had nothing to do with courtesy. They were men of power. It was only power that they dealt with. And what power had she now? What had she ever had? As a girl, a priestess, she had been a vessel: the power of the dark places had run through her, used her, left her empty, untouched. As a young woman she had been taught a powerful knowledge by a powerful man and had laid it aside, turned away from it, not touched it. As a woman she had chosen and had the powers of a woman, in their time, and the time was past; her wiving and mothering was done. There was nothing in her, no power, for anybody to recognize.

But a dragon had spoken to her. "I am Kalessin," it had said, and she had answered, "I am Tenar."

"What is a dragonlord?" she had asked Ged, in the dark place, the Labyrinth, trying to deny his power, trying to make him admit hers; and he had answered with the plain honesty that forever disarmed her, "A man dragons will talk to."

So she was a woman dragons would talk to. Was that the new thing, the folded knowledge, the light seed, that she felt in herself, waking beneath the small window that looked west?

A few days after that brief conversation at table, she was weeding Ogion's garden patch, rescuing the onions he had set out in spring from the weeds of summer. Ged let himself in the gate in the high fence that kept the goats out, and set to weeding at the other end of the row. He worked awhile and then sat back, looking down at his hands.

"Let them have time to heal," Tenar said mildly.

He nodded.

The tall staked bean-plants in the next row were flowering. Their scent was very sweet. He sat with his thin arms on his knees, staring into the sunlit tangle of vines and flowers and hanging beanpods. She spoke as she worked: "When Aihal died, he said, 'All changed. . . .' And since his death, I've mourned him, I've grieved, but something lifts up my grief. Something is coming to be born—has been set free. I know in my sleep and my first waking, something is changed."

"Yes," he said. "An evil ended. And . . ."

After a long silence he began again. He did not look at her, but his voice sounded for the first time like the voice she remembered, easy, quiet, with the dry Gontish accent.

"Do you remember, Tenar, when we came first to Havnor?"

Would I forget? her heart said, but she was silent for fear of driving him back into silence.

"We brought *Lookfar* in and came up onto the quai—the steps are marble. And the people, all the people—and you held up your arm to show them the Ring. . . ."

"—And held your hand; I was terrified beyond terror: the faces, the voices, the colors, the towers and the flags and banners, the gold and silver and music, and all I knew was you—in the whole world all I knew was you, there by me as we walked. . . ."

"The stewards of the King's House brought us to the foot of the Tower of Erreth-Akbe, through the streets full of people. And we went up the high steps, the two of us alone. Do you remember?"

She nodded. She laid her hands on the earth she had been weeding, feeling its grainy coolness.

"I opened the door. It was heavy, it stuck at first. And we went in. Do you remember?"

It was as if he asked for reassurance— Did it happen? Do I remember?

"It was a great, high hall," she said. "It made me think of my Hall, where I was eaten, but only because it was so high. The light came down from windows away up in the tower. Shafts of sunlight crossing like swords."

"And the throne," he said.

"The throne, yes, all gold and crimson. But empty. Like the throne in the Hall in Atuan."

"Not now," he said. He looked across the green shoots of onion at her. His face was strained, wistful, as if he named a joy he could not grasp. "There is a king in Havnor," he said, "at the center of the world. What was foretold has been fulfilled. The Rune is healed, and the world is whole. The days of peace have come. He—"

He stopped and looked down, clenching his hands.

"He carried me from death to life. Arren of Enlad. Lebannen of the songs to be sung. He has taken his true name, Lebannen, King of Earthsea."

"Is that it, then," she asked, kneeling, watching him—"the joy, the coming into light?"

He did not answer.

A king in Havnor, she thought, and said aloud, "A king in Havnor!"

The vision of the beautiful city was in her, the wide streets, the towers of marble, the tiled and bronze roofs, the white-sailed ships in harbor, the marvelous throne room where sunlight fell like swords, the wealth and dignity and harmony, the order that was kept there. From that bright center, she saw order going outward like the perfect rings on water, like the straightness of a paved street or a ship sailing before the wind: a going the way it should go, a bringing to peace.

"You did well, dear friend," she said.

He made a little gesture as if to stop her words, and then turned away, pressing his hand to his mouth. She could not bear to see his tears. She bent to her work. She pulled a weed, and another, and the tough root broke. She dug with her hands, trying to find the root of the weed in the harsh soil, in the dark of the earth.

"Goha," said Therru's weak, cracked voice at the gate, and Tenar looked round. The child's half-face looked straight at her from the seeing eye and the blinded eye. Tenar thought, Shall I tell her that there is a king in Havnor?

She got up and went to the gate to spare Therru from trying to make herself heard. When she lay in the fire unconscious, Beech said, the child had breathed in fire. "Her voice is burned away," he explained.

"I was watching Sippy," Therru whispered, "but she got out of the broom-pasture. I can't find her."

It was as long a speech as she had ever made. She was trembling from running and from trying not to cry. We can't all be weeping at once, Tenar said to herself—this is stupid, we can't have this!— "Sparrowhawk!" she said, turning, "there's a goat got out."

He stood up at once and came to the gate.

"Try the springhouse," he said.

He looked at Therru as if he did not see her hideous scars, as if he scarcely saw her at all: a child who had lost a goat, who needed to find a goat. It was the goat he saw. "Or she's off to join the village flock," he said.

Therru was already running to the springhouse.

"Is she your daughter?" he asked Tenar. He had never before said a word about the child, and all Tenar could think for a moment was how very strange men were.

"No, nor my granddaughter. But my child," she said. What was it that made her jeer at him, jibe at him, again?

He let himself out the gate, just as Sippy dashed toward them, a brown-and-white flash, followed far behind by Therru.

"Hi!" Ged shouted suddenly, and with a leap he blocked the goat's way, heading her directly to the open gate and Tenar's arms. She managed to grab Sippy's loose leather collar. The goat at once stood still, mild as any lamb, looking at Tenar with one yellow eye and at the onion-rows with the other.

"Out," said Tenar, leading her out of goat heaven and over to the stonier pasture where she was supposed to be.

Ged had sat down on the ground, as out of breath as Therru, or more so, for he gasped, and was evidently dizzy; but at least he was not in tears. Trust a goat to spoil anything.

"Heather shouldn't have told you to watch Sippy," Tenar said to Therru. "Nobody can watch Sippy. If she gets out again, tell Heather, and don't worry. All right?"

Therru nodded. She was looking at Ged. She seldom looked at people, and very seldom at men, for longer than a glance; but she was gazing at him steadily, her head cocked like a sparrow. Was a hero being born?

WORSENING

IT WAS WELL OVER A MONTH SINCE the solstice, but the evenings were still long up on the west-facing Overfell. Therru had come in late from an all-day herbal expedition with Aunty Moss, too tired to eat. Tenar put her to bed and sat with her, singing to her. When the child was overtired she could not sleep, but would crouch in the bed like a paralyzed animal, staring at hallucinations till she was in a nightmare state, neither sleeping nor waking, and unreachable. Tenar had found she could prevent this by holding her and singing her to sleep. When she ran out of the songs she had learned as a farmer's wife in Middle Valley, she sang interminable Kargish chants she had learned as a child priestess at the Tombs of Atuan, lulling Therru with the drone and sweet whine of offerings to the

Nameless Powers and the Empty Throne that was now filled with the dust and ruin of earthquake. She felt no power in those songs but that of song itself; and she liked to sing in her own language, though she did not know the songs a mother would sing to a child in Atuan, the songs her mother had sung to her.

Therru was fast asleep at last. Tenar slipped her from her lap to the bed and waited a moment to be sure she slept on. Then, after a glance round to be sure she was alone, with an almost guilty quickness, yet with the ceremony of enjoyment, of great pleasure, she laid her narrow, light-skinned hand along the side of the child's face where eye and cheek had been eaten away by fire, leaving slabbed, bald scar. Under her touch all that was gone. The flesh was whole, a child's round, soft, sleeping face. It was as if her touch restored the truth.

Lightly, reluctantly, she lifted her palm, and saw the irremediable loss, the healing that would never be whole.

She bent down and kissed the scar, got up quietly, and went out of the house.

The sun was setting in a vast, pearly haze. No one was about. Sparrowhawk was probably off in the forest. He had begun to visit Ogion's grave, spending hours in that quiet place under the beech tree, and as he got more strength he took to wandering on up the forest paths that Ogion had loved. Food evidently had no savor to him; Tenar had to ask him to eat. Companionship he shunned, seeking only to be alone. Therru would have followed him anywhere, and being as silent as he was she did not trouble him, but he was restless, and presently would send the child home and go on by himself, farther, to what ends Tenar did not know. He would come in late, cast himself down to sleep, and often be gone again before she and the child woke. She would leave him bread and meat to take with him.

She saw him now coming along the meadow path that had been so long and hard when she had helped Ogion walk it for the last time. He came through the luminous air, the wind-bowed grasses, walking steadily, locked in his obstinate misery, hard as stone.

"Will you be about the house?" she asked him, across some distance. "Therru's asleep. I want to walk a little."

"Yes. Go on," he said, and she went on, pondering the indifference of a man towards the exigencies that ruled a woman: that someone must be not far from a sleeping child, that one's freedom meant another's unfreedom, unless some ever-changing, moving balance were reached, like the balance of a body moving forward, as she did now, on two legs, first one then the other, in the practice of that remarkable art, walking. . . . Then the deepening colors of the sky and the soft insistence of the wind replaced her thoughts. She went on walking, without metaphors, until she came to the sandstone cliffs. There she stopped and watched the sun be lost in the serene, rosy haze.

She knelt and found with her eyes and then with her fingertips a long, shallow, blurred groove in the rock, scored right out to the edge of the cliff: the track of Kalessin's tail. She followed it again and again with her fingers, gazing out into the gulfs of twilight, dreaming. She spoke once. The name was not fire in her mouth this time, but hissed and dragged softly out of her lips, "Kalessin. . . ."

She looked up to the east. The summits of Gont Mountain above the forests were red, catching the light that was gone here below. The color dimmed as she watched. She looked away and when she looked back the summit was grey, obscure, the forested slopes dark.

She waited for the evening star. When it shone above the haze, she walked slowly home.

Home, not home. Why was she here in Ogion's house not in her own farmhouse, looking after Ogion's goats and onions not her own orchards and flocks? "Wait," he had said, and she had waited; and the dragon had come; and Ged was well now—was well enough. She had done her part. She had kept the house. She was no longer needed. It was time she left.

Yet she could not think of leaving this high ledge, this hawk's nest, and going down into the lowlands again, the easy farmlands, the windless inlands, she could not think of that without her heart sinking and darkening. What of the dream she had here, under the small window looking west? What of the dragon who had come to her here?

The door of the house stood open as usual for light and air. Sparrowhawk was sitting without lamp or firelight on a low seat by the swept hearth. He often sat there. She thought it had been his place when he was a boy here, in his brief apprenticeship with Ogion. It had been her place, winter days, when she had been Ogion's pupil.

He looked at her entering, but his eyes had not been on the doorway but beside it to the right, the dark corner behind the door. Ogion's staff stood there, an oaken stick, heavy, worn smooth at the grip, the height of the man himself. Beside it Therru had set the hazel switch and the alder stick Tenar had cut for them when they were walking to Re Albi.

Tenar thought—His staff, his wizard's staff, yew-wood, Ogion gave it to him— Where is it?— And at the same time, Why have I not thought of that till now?

It was dark in the house, and seemed stuffy. She was oppressed. She had wished he would stay to talk with her, but now that he sat there she had nothing to say to him, nor he to her.

"I've been thinking," she said at last, setting straight the four dishes on the oaken sideboard, "that it's time I was getting back to my farm."

He said nothing. Possibly he nodded, but her back was turned.

She was tired all at once, wanting to go to bed; but he sat there in the front part of the house, and it was not yet entirely dark; she could not undress in front of him. Shame made her angry. She was about to ask him to go out for while when he spoke, clearing his throat, hesitant.

"The books. Ogion's books. The Runes and the two Lore-books. Would you be taking them with you?"

"With me?"

"You were his last student."

She came over to the hearth and sat down across from him on Ogion's three-legged chair.

"I learned to write the runes of Hardic, but I've forgotten most of that, no doubt. He taught me some of the language the dragons speak. Some of that I remember. But nothing else. I didn't become an adept, a wizard. I got married, you know. Would Ogion have left his books of wisdom to a farmer's wife?"

After a pause he said without expression, "Did he not leave them to someone, then?"

"To you, surely."

Sparrowhawk said nothing.

"You were his last prentice, and his pride, and friend. He never said it, but of course they go to you."

"What am I to do with them?"

She stared at him through the dusk. The western window gleamed faint across the room. The dour, relentless, unexplaining rage in his voice roused her own anger.

"You the Archmage ask me? Why do you make a worse fool of me than I am, Ged?"

He got up then. His voice shook. "But don't you—can't you see—all that is over—is gone!"

She sat staring, trying to see his face.

"I have no power, nothing. I gave it—spent it— all I had. To close— So that— So it's done, done with."

She tried to deny what he said, but could not.

"Like pouring out a little water," he said, "a cup of water onto the sand. In the dry land. I had to do that. But now I have nothing to drink. And what difference, what difference did it make, does it make, one cup of water in all the desert? Is the desert gone?—Ah! Listen!—It used to whisper that to me from behind the door there: Listen, listen! And I went into the dry land when I was young. And I met it there, I became it, I married my death. It gave me life. Water, the water of life. I was a foun- tain, a spring, flowing, giving. But the springs don't run, there. All I had in the end was one cup of water, and I had to pour it out on the sand, in the bed of the dry river, on the rocks in the dark. So it's gone. It's over. Done."

She knew enough, from Ogion and from Ged himself, to know what land he spoke of, and that though he spoke in images they were not masks of the truth but the truth itself as he had known it. She knew also that she must deny what he said, no matter if it was true. "You don't give yourself time, Ged," she said. "Coming back from death must be a long journey—even on the dragon's back. It will take time. Time and quiet, silence, stillness. You have been hurt. You will be healed."

For a long while he was silent, standing there. She thought she had said the right thing, and given him some comfort. But he spoke at last.

"Like the child?"

It was like a knife so sharp she did not feel it come into her body.

"I don't know," he said in the same soft, dry voice, "why you took her, knowing that she cannot be healed. Knowing what her life must be. I suppose it's a part of this time we have lived—a dark time, an age of ruin, an ending time. You took her, I suppose, as I went to meet my enemy, because it was all you could do. And so we must live on into the new age with the spoils of our victory over evil. You with your burned child, and I with nothing at all."

Despair speaks evenly, in a quiet voice.

Tenar turned to look at the mage's staff in the dark place to the right of the door, but there was no light in it. It was all dark, inside and out. Through the open doorway a couple of stars were visible, high and faint. She looked at them. She wanted to know what stars they were. She got up and went groping past the table to the door. The haze had risen and not many stars were visible. One of those she had seen from indoors was the white summer star that they called, in Atuan, in her own language, Tehanu. She did not know the other one. She did not know what they called Tehanu here, in Hardic, or what its true name was, what the dragons called it. She knew only what her mother would have called it, Tehanu, Tehanu. Tenar, Tenar . . .

"Ged," she said from the doorway, not turning, "who brought you up, when you were a child?"

He came to stand near her, also looking out at the misty horizon of the sea, the stars, the dark bulk of the mountain above them.

"Nobody much," he said. "My mother died when I was a baby. There were some older brothers. I don't remember them. There was my father the smith. And my mother's sister. She was the witch of Ten Alders."

"Aunty Moss," Tenar said.

"Younger. She had some power."

"What was her name?"

He was silent.

"I cannot remember," he said slowly.

After a while he said, "She taught me the names. Falcon, pilgrim falcon, eagle, osprey, goshawk, sparrowhawk. . . ."

"What do you call that star? The white one, up high."

"The Heart of the Swan," he said, looking up at it. "In Ten Alders they called it the Arrow."

But he did not say its name in the Language of the Making, nor the true names the witch had taught him of hawk, falcon, sparrowhawk.

"What I said—in there—was wrong," he said softly. "I shouldn't speak at all. Forgive me."

"If you won't speak, what can I do but leave you?" She turned to him. "Why do you think only of yourself? Always of yourself? Go outside awhile," she told him, wrathful. "I want to go to bed."

Bewildered, muttering some apology, he went out; and she, going to the alcove, slipped out of her clothes and into the bed, and hid her face in the sweet warmth of Therru's silky nape.

"Knowing what her life must be . . ."

Her anger with him, her stupid denial of the truth of what he told her, rose from disappointment. Though Lark had said ten times over that nothing could be done, yet she had hoped that Tenar could heal the burns; and for all her saying that even Ogion could not have done it, Tenar had hoped that Ged could heal Therru—could lay his hand on the scar and it would be whole and well, the blind eye bright, the clawed hand soft, the ruined life intact.

"Knowing what her life must be . . ."

The averted faces, the signs against evil, the horror and curiosity, the sickly pity and the prying threat, for harm draws harm to it . . . And never a man's arms. Never anyone to hold her. Never anyone but Tenar. Oh, he was right, the child should have died, should be dead. They should have let her go into that dry land, she and Lark and Ivy, meddling old women, softhearted and cruel. He was right, he was always right. But then, the men who had used her for their needs and games, the woman who had suffered her to be used—they had been quite right to beat her unconscious and push her into the fire to burn to death. Only they had not been thorough. They had lost their nerve, they had left some life in her. That had been wrong. And everything she, Tenar, had done was wrong. She had been given to the dark powers as a child: she had been eaten by them, she had been suffered to be eaten. Did she think that by crossing the sea, by learning other languages, by being a man's wife, a mother of children, that by merely living her life, she could ever be anything but what she was—their servant, their food, theirs to use for their needs and games? Destroyed, she had drawn the destroyed to her, part of her own ruin, the body of her own evil.

The child's hair was fine, warm, sweet-smelling. She lay curled up in the warmth of Tenar's arms, dreaming. What wrong could she be? Wronged, wronged beyond all repair, but not wrong. Not lost, not lost, not lost. Tenar held her and lay still and set her mind on the light of her dreaming, the gulfs of bright air, the name of the dragon, the name of the star, Heart of the Swan, the Arrow, Tehanu.

She was combing the black goat for the fine underwool that she would spin and take to a weaver to make into cloth, the silky "fleecefell" of Gont Island. The old black goat had been combed a thousand times, and liked it, leaning into the dig and pull of the wire comb-teeth. The grey-black combings grew into a soft, dirty cloud, which Tenar at last stuffed into a net bag; she worked some burrs out of the fringes of the goat's ears by way of thanks, and slapped her barrel flank companionably. "Bah!" the goat said, and trotted off. Tenar let herself out of the fenced pasture and came around in front of the house, glancing over the meadow to make sure Therru was still playing there.

Moss had shown the child how to weave grass baskets, and clumsy as her crippled hand was, she had begun to get the trick of it. She sat there in the meadow grass with her work on her lap, but she was not working. She was watching Sparrowhawk.

He stood a good way off, nearer the cliff's edge. His back was turned, and he did not know anyone was watching him, for he was watching a bird, a young kestrel; and she in turn was watching some small prey she had glimpsed in the grass. She hung beating her wings, wanting to flush the vole or mouse, to panic it into a rush to its nest. The man stood, as intent, as hungry, gazing at the bird. Slowly he lifted his right hand, holding the forearm level, and he seemed to speak, though the wind bore his words away. The kestrel veered, crying her high, harsh, keening cry, and shot up and off toward the forests.

The man lowered his arm and stood still, watching the bird. The child and the woman were still. Only the bird flew, went free.

"He came to me once as a falcon, a pilgrim falcon," Ogion had said, by the fire, on a winter day. He had been telling her of the spells of Changing, of transformations, of the mage Bordger who had become a bear. "He flew to me, to my wrist, out of the north and west. I brought him in by the fire here. He could not speak. Because I knew him, I was able to help him; he could put off the falcon, and be a man again. But there was always some hawk in him. They called him Sparrowhawk in his village because the wild hawks would come to him, at his word. Who are we? What is it to be a man? Before he had his name, before he had knowledge, before he had power, the hawk was in him, and the man, and the mage, and more—he was what we cannot name. And so are we all."

The girl sitting at the hearth, gazing at the fire, listening, saw the hawk; saw the man; saw the birds come to him, come at his word, at his naming them, come beating their wings to hold his arm with their fierce talons; saw herself the hawk, the wild bird.

ᏌICE

TOWNSEND, THE SHEEP-BUYER WHO had brought Ogion's message to the farm in Middle Valley, came out one afternoon to the mage's house.

"Will you be selling the goats, now Lord Ogion's gone?"

"I might," Tenar said neutrally. She had in fact been wondering how, if she stayed in Re Albi, she would get on. Like any wizard, Ogion had been supported by the people his skills and powers served—in his case, anyone on Gont. He had only to ask and what he needed would be given gratefully, a good bargain for the goodwill of a mage; but he never had to ask. Rather he had to give away the excess of food and raiment and tools and livestock and all necessities and ornaments that were offered or simply left on his doorstep. "What shall I do with them?" he would demand, perplexed, standing with his arms full of indignant, squawking chickens, or yards of tapestry, or pots of pickled beets.

But Tenar had left her living in the Middle Valley. She had not thought when she left so suddenly of how long she might stay. She had not brought with her the seven pieces of ivory, Flint's hoard; nor would that money have been of use in the village except to buy land or livestock, or deal with some trader up from Gont Port peddling pellawi furs or silks of Lorbanery to the rich farmers and little lords of Gont. Flint's farm gave her all she and Therru needed to eat and wear; but Ogion's six goats and his beans and onions had been for his pleasure rather than his need. She had been living off his larder, the gifts of villagers who gave to her for his sake, and the generosity of Aunty Moss. Just yesterday the witch had said, "Dearie, my ringneck hen's brood's hatched out, and I'll bring you two-three chickies when they begin to scratch. The mage wouldn't keep 'em, too noisy and silly, he said, but what's a house without chickies at the door?"

Indeed her hens wandered in and out of Moss's door freely, and slept on her bed, and enriched the smells of the dark, smoky, reeking room beyond belief.

"There's a brown-and-white yearling nanny will make a fine milch goat," Tenar said to the sharp-faced man.

"I was thinking of the whole lot," he said.

"Maybe. Only five or six of 'em, right?"

"Six. They're in the pasture up there if you want to have a look."

"I'll do that." But he didn't move. No eagerness, of course, was to be evinced on either side.

"Seen the great ship come in?" he asked.

Ogion's house looked west and north, and from it one could see only the rocky headlands at the mouth of the bay, the Armed Cliffs; but from the village itself at several places one could look down the steep back-and-forth road to Gont Port and see the docks and the whole harbor. Shipwatching was a regular pursuit in Re Albi. There were generally a couple of old men on the bench behind the smithy, which gave the best view, and though they might never in their lives have gone down the fifteen zigzag miles of that road to Gont Port, they watched the comings and goings of ships as a spectacle, strange yet familiar, provided for their entertainment.

"From Havnor, smith's boy said. He was down in Port bargaining for ingots. Come up yesterevening late. The great ship's from Havnor Great Port, he said."

He was probably talking to keep her mind off the price of goats, and the slyness of his look was probably simply the way his eyes were made. But Havnor Great Port traded little with Gont, a poor and remote island notable only for wizards, pirates, and goats; and something in the words, "the great ship," troubled or alarmed her, she did not know why.

"He said they say there's a king in Havnor now," the sheep-buyer went on, with a sidelong glance.

"That might be a good thing," said Tenar.

Townsend nodded. "Might keep the foreign riffraff out."

Tenar nodded her foreign head pleasantly.

"But there's those down in Port won't be pleased, maybe." He meant the pirate sea-captains of Gont, whose control of the northeastern seas had been increasing of late years to the point where many of the old trade-schedules with the central islands of the Archipelago had been disrupted or abandoned; this impoverished everyone on Gont except the pirates, but that did not prevent the pirates from being heroes in the eyes of most Gontishmen. For all she knew, Tenar's son was a sailor on a pirate ship. And safer, maybe, as such than on a steady merchantman. *Better shark than herring,* as they said.

"There's some who're never pleased no matter what," Tenar said, automatically following the rules of conversation, but impatient enough with them that she added, rising, "I'll show you the goats. You can have a look. I don't know if we'll sell all or any." And she took the man to the broom-pasture gate and left him. She did not like him. It wasn't his fault that he had brought her bad news once and maybe twice, but his eyes slid, and she did not like his company. She wouldn't sell him Ogion's goats. Not even Sippy.

After he had left, bargainless, she found herself uneasy. She had said to him, "I don't know if we'll sell," and that had been foolish, to say *we* instead of *I*, when he hadn't asked to speak to Sparrowhawk, hadn't even alluded to him, as a man bargaining with a woman was more than likely to do, especially when she was refusing his offer.

She did not know what they made of Sparrowhawk, of his presence and nonpresence, in the village. Ogion, aloof and silent and in some ways feared, had been their own mage and their fellow-villager. Sparrowhawk they might be proud of as a name, the archmage who had lived awhile in Re Albi and done wonderful things, fooling a dragon in the Ninety Isles, bringing the Ring of Erreth-Akbe back from somewhere or other; but they did not know him. Nor did he know them. He had not gone into the village since he came, only to the forest, the wilderness. She had not thought about it before, but he avoided the village as surely as Therru did.

They must have talked about him. It was a village, and people talked. But gossip about the doings of wizards and mages would not go far. The matter was too uncanny, the lives of men of power were too strange, too different from their own. "Let be," she had heard villagers in the Middle Valley say when somebody got to speculating too freely about a visiting weatherworker or their own wizard, Beech— "Let be. He goes his way, not ours."

As for herself, that she should have stayed on to nurse and serve such a man of power would not seem a questionable matter to them; again it was a case of "Let be." She had not been very much in the village herself; they were neither friendly nor unfriendly to her. She had lived there once in Weaver Fan's cottage, she was the old mage's ward, he had sent Townsend down round the mountain for her; all that was very well. But then she had come with the child, terrible to look at, who'd walk about in daylight with it by choice? And what kind of woman would be a wizard's pupil, a wizard's nurse? Witchery there, sure enough, and foreign too. But all the same, she was wife to a rich farmer way down there in the Middle Valley; though he was dead and she a widow. Well, who could understand the ways of the witchfolk? Let be, better let be. . . .

She met the Archmage of Earthsea as he came past the garden fence. She said, "They say there's a ship in from the City of Havnor."

He stopped. He made a movement, quickly controlled, but it had been the beginning of a turn to run, to break and run like a mouse from a hawk.

"Ged!" she said. "What is it?"

"I can't," he said. "I can't face them."

"Who?"

"Men from him. From the king."

His face had gone greyish, as when he was first here, and he looked around for a place to hide.

His terror was so urgent and undefended that she thought only how to spare him. "You needn't see them. If anybody comes I'll send them away. Come back to the house now. You haven't eaten all day."

"There was a man there," he said.

"Townsend, pricing goats. I sent *him* away. Come on!"

He came with her, and when they were in the house she shut the door.

"They couldn't harm you, surely, Ged. Why would they want to?"

He sat down at the table and shook his head dully. "No, no."

"Do they know you're here?"

"I don't know."

"What is it you're afraid of?" she asked, not impatiently, but with some rational authority.

He put his hands across his face, rubbing his temples and forehead, looking down. "I was—" he said. "I'm not—"

It was all he could say.

She stopped him, saying, "All right, it's all right." She dared not touch him lest she worsen his humiliation by any semblance of pity. She was angry at him, and for him. "It's none of their business," she said, "where you are, or who you are, or what you choose to do or not to do! If they come prying they can leave curious." That was Lark's saying. She had a pang of longing for the company of an ordinary, sensible woman. "Anyhow, the ship may have nothing at all to do with you. They may be chasing pirates home. It'll be a good thing, too, when the king gets around to doing that. . . . I found some wine in the back of the cupboard, a couple of bottles, I wonder how long Ogion had it squirreled away there. I think we'd both do well with a glass of wine. And some bread and cheese. The little one's had her dinner and gone off with Heather to catch frogs. There may be frogs' legs for supper. But bread and cheese for now. And wine. I wonder where it's from, who brought it to Ogion, how old it is?" So she talked along, woman's babble, saving him from having to make any answer or misread any silence, until he had got over the crisis of shame, and eaten a little, and drunk a glass of the old, soft, red wine.

"It's best I go, Tenar," he said. "Till I learn to be what I am now."

"Go where?"

"Up on the mountain."

"Wandering—like Ogion?" She looked at him. She remembered walking with him on the roads of Atuan, deriding him: "Do wizards often beg?" And he had answered, "Yes, but they try to give something in exchange."

She asked cautiously, "Could you get on for a while as a weatherworker, or a finder?" She filled his glass full.

He shook his head. He drank wine, and looked

away. "No," he said. "None of that. Nothing of that."

She did not believe him. She wanted to rebel, to deny, to say to him, How can it be, how can you say that—as if you'd forgotten all you know, all you learned from Ogion, and at Roke, and in your traveling! You can't have forgotten the words, the names, the acts of your art. You learned, you earned your power!—She kept herself from saying that, but she murmured, "I don't understand. How can it all . . ."

"A cup of water," he said, tipping his glass a little as if to pour it out. And after a while, "What I don't understand is why he brought me back. The kindness of the young is cruelty. . . . So I'm here, I have to get on with it, till I can go back."

She did not know clearly what he meant, but she heard a note of blame or complaint that, in him, shocked and angered her. She spoke stiffly: "It was Kalessin that brought you here."

It was dark in the house with the door closed and only the small western window letting in the late-afternoon light. She could not make out his expression; but presently he raised his glass to her with a shadowy smile, and drank.

"This wine," he said. "Some great merchant or pirate must have brought it to Ogion. I never drank its equal. Even in Havnor." He turned the squat glass in his hands, looking down at it. "I'll call myself something," he said, "and go across the mountain, to Armouth and the East Forest country, where I came from. They'll be making hay. There's always work at haying and harvest."

She did not know how to answer. Fragile and ill-looking, he would be given such work only out of charity or brutality; and if he got it he would not be able to do it.

"The roads aren't like they used to be," she said. "These last years, there's thieves and gangs everywhere. Foreign riffraff, as my friend Townsend says. But it's not safe any more to go alone."

Looking at him in the dusky light to see how he took this, she wondered sharply for a moment what it must be like never to have feared a human being—what it would be like to have to learn to be afraid.

"Ogion still went—" he began, and then set his mouth; he had recalled that Ogion had been a mage.

"Down in the south part of the island," Tenar said, "there's a lot of herding. Sheep, goats, cattle. They drive them up into the hills before the Long Dance, and pasture them there until the rains. They're always needing herders." She drank a mouthful of the wine. It was like the dragon's name in her mouth. "But why can't you just stay here?"

"Not in Ogion's house. The first place they'll come."

"Well, what if they do come? What will they want of you?"

"To be what I was."

The desolation of his voice chilled her.

She was silent, trying to remember what it was like to have been powerful, to be the Eaten One, the One Priestess of the Tombs of Atuan, and then to lose that, throw it away, become only Tenar, only herself. She thought about how it was to have been a woman in the prime of life, with children and a man, and then to lose all that, becoming old and a widow, powerless. But even so she did not feel she understood his shame, his agony of humiliation. Perhaps only a man could feel so. A woman got used to shame.

Or maybe Aunty Moss was right, and when the meat was out the shell was empty.

Witch-thoughts, she thought. And to turn his mind and her own, and because the soft, fiery wine made her wits and tongue quick, she said, "Do you know, I've thought—about Ogion teaching me, and I wouldn't go on, but went and found myself my farmer and married him—I thought, when I did that, I thought on my wedding day, Ged will be angry when he hears of this!" She laughed as she spoke.

"I was," he said.

She waited.

He said, "I was disappointed."

"Angry," she said.

"Angry," he said.

He poured her glass full.

"I had the power to know power, then," he said. "And you—you shone, in that terrible place, the Labyrinth, that darkness. . . ."

"Well, then, tell me: what should I have done with my power, and the knowledge Ogion tried to teach me?"

"Use it."

"How?"

"As the Art Magic is used."

"By whom?"

"Wizards," he said, a little painfully.

"Magic means the skills, the arts of wizards, of mages?"

"What else would it mean?"

"Is that all it could ever mean?"

He pondered, glancing up at her once or twice.

"When Ogion taught me," she said, "here—at the hearth there—the words of the Old Speech, they were as easy and as hard in my mouth as in his. That was like learning the language I spoke before I was born. But the rest—the lore, the runes of power, the spells, the rules, the raising of the forces—that was all dead to me. Somebody else's language. I used to think, I could be dressed up as a warrior, with a lance and a sword and a plume and all, but it wouldn't fit, would it? What would I do with the sword? Would it make me a hero? I'd be myself in clothes that didn't fit, is all, hardly able to walk."

She sipped her wine.

"So I took it all off," she said, "and put on my own clothes."

"What did Ogion say when you left him?"

"What did Ogion usually say?"

That roused the shadowy smile again. He said nothing.

She nodded.

After a while, she went on more softly, "He took me because you brought me to him. He wanted no prentice after you, and he never would have taken a girl but from you, at your asking. But he loved me. He did me honor. And I loved and honored him. But he couldn't give me what I wanted, and I couldn't take what he had to give me. He knew that. But, Ged, it was a different matter when he saw Therru. The day before he died. You say, and Moss says, that power knows power. I don't know what he saw in her, but he said, 'Teach her!' And he said . . ."

Ged waited.

"He said, 'They will fear her.' And he said, 'Teach her *all!* Not Roke.' I don't know what he meant. How can I know? If I had stayed here with him I might know, I might be able to teach her. But I thought, Ged will come, he'll know. He'll know what to teach her, what she needs to know, my wronged one."

"I do not know," he said, speaking very low. "I saw—In the child I see only—the wrong done. The evil."

He drank off his wine.

"I have nothing to give her," he said.

There was a little scraping knock at the door. He started up instantly with that same helpless turn of the body, looking for a place to hide.

Tenar went to the door, opened it a crack, and smelled Moss before she saw her.

"Men in the village," the old woman whispered dramatically. "All kind of fine folk come up from the Port, from the great ship that's in from Havnor City, they say. Come after the Archmage, they say."

"He doesn't want to see them," Tenar said weakly. She had no idea what to do.

"I dare say not," said the witch. And after an expectant pause, "Where is he, then?"

"Here," said Sparrowhawk, coming to the door and opening it wider. Moss eyed him and said nothing.

"Do they know where I am?"

"Not from me," Moss said.

"If they come here," said Tenar, "all you have to do is send them away—after all, you are the Archmage—"

Neither he nor Moss was paying attention to her.

"They won't come to *my* house," Moss said. "Come on, if you like."

He followed her, with a glance but no word to Tenar.

"But what am I to tell them?" she demanded.

"Nothing, dearie," said the witch.

Heather and Therru came back from the marshes with seven dead frogs in a net bag, and Tenar busied herself cutting off and skinning the legs for the hunters' supper. She was just finishing when she heard voices outside, and looking up at the open door saw people standing at it—men in hats, a twist of gold, a glitter— "Mistress Goha?" said a civil voice.

"Come in!" she said.

They came in: five men, seeming twice as many in the low-ceilinged room, and tall, and grand. They looked about them, and she saw what they saw.

They saw a woman standing at a table, holding a long, sharp knife. On the table was a chopping board and on that, to one side, a little heap of naked greenish-white legs; to the other, a heap of fat, bloody, dead frogs. In the shadow behind the door something lurked—a child, but a child deformed, mismade, half-faced, claw-handed. On a bed in an alcove beneath the single window sat a big, bony young woman, staring at them with her mouth wide open. Her hands were bloody and muddy and her dank skirt smelled of marsh-water. When she saw them look at her, she tried to hide her face with her skirt, baring her legs to the thigh.

They looked away from her, and from the child, and there was no one else to look at but the woman with the dead frogs.

"Mistress Goha," one of them repeated.

"So I'm called," she said.

"We come from Havnor, from the King," said the civil voice. She could not see his face clearly against the light. "We seek the Archmage, Sparrowhawk of Gont. King Lebannen is to be crowned at the turn of autumn, and he seeks to have the Archmage, his lord and friend, with him to make ready for the coronation, and to crown him, if he will."

The man spoke steadily and formally, as to a lady in a palace. He wore sober breeches of leather and a linen shirt dusty from the climb up from Gont Port, but it was fine cloth, with embroidery of gold thread at the throat.

"He's not here," Tenar said.

A couple of little boys from the village peered in at the door and drew back, peered again, fled shouting.

"Maybe you can tell us where he is, Mistress Goha," said the man.

"I cannot."

She looked at them all. The fear of them she had felt at first—caught from Sparrowhawk's panic, perhaps, or mere foolish fluster at seeing strangers—was subsiding. Here she stood in Ogion's house; and she knew well enough why Ogion had never been afraid of great people.

"You must be tired after that long road," she said. "Will you sit down? There's wine. Here, I must wash the glasses."

She carried the chopping board over to the sideboard, put the frogs' legs in the larder, scraped the rest into the swill-pail that Heather would carry to Weaver Fan's pigs, washed her hands and arms and the knife at the basin, poured fresh water, and rinsed out the two glasses she and Sparrowhawk had drunk from. There was one other glass in the cabinet, and two clay cups without handles. She set these on the table, and poured wine for the visitors; there was just enough left in the bottle to go round. They had exchanged glances, and had not sat down. The shortage of chairs excused that. The rules of hospitality, however, bound them to accept what she offered. Each man took glass or cup from her with a polite murmur. Saluting her, they drank.

"My word!" said one of them.

"Andrades—the Late Harvest," said another, with round eyes.

A third shook his head. "Andrades—the Dragon Year," he said solemnly.

The fourth nodded and sipped again, reverent.

The fifth, who was the first to have spoken, lifted his clay cup to Tenar again and said, "You honor us with a king's wine, mistress."

"It was Ogion's," she said. "This was Ogion's house. This is Aihal's house. You knew that, my lords?"

"We did, mistress. The king sent us to this house, believing that the archmage would come here; and, when word of the death of its master came to Roke and Havnor, yet more certain of it. But it was a dragon that bore the archmage from Roke. And no word or sending has come from him since then to Roke or to the king. And it is much in the king's heart, and much in the interest of us all, to know the archmage is here, and is well. Did he come here, mistress?"

"I cannot say," she said, but it was a poor equivocation, repeated, and she could see that the men thought so. She drew herself up, standing behind the table. "I mean that I will not say. I think if the archmage wishes to come, he will come. If he wishes not to be found, you will not find him. Surely you will not seek him out against his will."

The oldest of the men, and the tallest, said, "The king's will is ours."

The first speaker said more conciliatingly, "We are only messengers. What is between the king and the archmage of the Isles is between them. We seek only to bring the message, and the reply."

"If I can, I will see that your message reaches him."

"And the reply?" the oldest man demanded.

She said nothing, and the first speaker said, "We'll be here some few days at the house of the Lord of Re Albi, who, hearing of our ship's arrival, offered us his hospitality."

She felt a sense of a trap laid or a noose tightening, though she did not know why. Sparrowhawk's vulnerability, his sense of his own weakness, had infected her. Distraught, she used the defense of her appearance, her seeming to be a mere goodwife, a middle-aged housekeeper—but was it seeming? It was also truth, and these matters were more subtle even than the guises and shape-changes of wizards.—She ducked her head and said, "That will be more befitting your lordships' comfort. You see we live very plain here, as the old mage did."

"And drink Andrades wine," said the one who had identified the vintage, a bright-eyed, handsome man with a winning smile. She, playing her part, kept her head down. But as they took their leave and filed out, she knew that, seem what she might and be what she might, if they did not know now that she was Tenar of the Ring they would know it soon enough; and so would know that she herself knew the archmage and was indeed their way to him, if they were determined to seek him out.

When they were gone, she heaved a great sigh. Heather did so too, and then finally shut her mouth, which had hung open all the time they were there.

"I never," she said, in a tone of deep, replete satisfaction, and went to see where the goats had got to.

Therru came out from the dark place behind the door, where she had barricaded herself from the strangers with Ogion's staff and Tenar's alder stick and her own hazel switch. She moved in the tight, sidling way she had mostly abandoned since they had been here, not looking up, the ruined half of her face bent down towards the shoulder.

Tenar went to her and knelt to hold her in her arms. "Therru," she said, "they won't hurt you. They mean no harm."

The child would not look at her. She let Tenar hold her like a block of wood.

"If you say so, I won't let them in the house again."

After a while the child moved a little and asked in her hoarse, thick voice, "What will they do to Sparrowhawk?"

"Nothing," Tenar said. "No harm! They come— they mean to do him honor."

But she had begun to see what their attempt to do him honor would do to him—denying his loss, denying him his grief for what he had lost, forcing him to act the part of what he was no longer.

When she let the child go, Therru went to the closet and fetched out Ogion's broom. She laboriously swept the floor where the men from Havnor had stood, sweeping away their footprints, sweeping the dust of their feet out the door, off the doorstep.

Watching her, Tenar made up her mind.

She went to the shelf where Ogion's three great books stood, and rummaged there. She found several goose quills and a half-dried-up bottle of ink, but not a scrap of paper or parchment. She set her jaw, hating to do damage to anything so sacred as a book, and scored and tore out a thin strip of paper from the blank endsheet of the Book of Runes. She sat at the table and dipped the pen and wrote. Neither the ink nor the words came easy. She had scarcely written anything since she had sat at this same table a quarter of a century ago, with Ogion looking over her shoulder, teaching her the runes of

Hardic and the Great Runes of Power. She wrote:

> go oak farm in midl valy to clerbrook
> say goha sent to look to garden & sheep

It took her nearly as long to read it over as it had to write it. By now Therru had finished her sweeping and was watching her, intent.

She added one word:

> to-night

"Where's Heather?" she asked the child, as she folded the paper on itself once and twice. "I want her to take this to Aunty Moss's house."

She longed to go herself, to see Sparrowhawk, but dared not be seen going, lest they were watching her to lead them to him.

"I'll go," Therru whispered.

Tenar looked at her sharply.

"You'll have to go alone, Therru. Past the village."

The child nodded.

"Give it only to him!"

She nodded again.

Tenar tucked the paper into the child's pocket, held her, kissed her, let her go. Therru went, not crouching and sidling now but running freely, flying, Tenar thought, seeing her vanish in the evening light beyond the dark door-frame, flying like a bird, a dragon, a child, free.

HAWKS

THERRU WAS BACK SOON WITH Sparrowhawk's reply: "He said he'll leave tonight."

Tenar heard this with satisfaction, relieved that he had accepted her plan, that he would get clear away from these messengers and messages he dreaded. It was not till she had fed Heather and Therru their frog-leg feast, and put Therru to bed and sung to her, and was sitting up alone without lamp or firelight, that her heart began to sink. He was gone. He was not strong, he was bewildered and uncertain, he needed friends; and she had sent him away from those who were and those who wished to be his friends. He was gone, and she must stay, to keep the hounds from his trail, to learn at least whether they stayed in Gont or sailed back to Havnor.

His panic and her obedience to it began to seem so unreasonable to her that she thought it equally unreasonable, improbable, that he would in fact go. He would use his wits and simply hide in Moss's house, which was the last place in all Earthsea that a king would look for an archmage. It would be much better if he stayed there till the king's men left. Then he could come back here to Ogion's house, where he belonged. And it would go on as before, she looking after him until he had his strength back, and he giving her his dear companionship.

A shadow against the stars in the doorway: "Hssssst! Awake?" Aunty Moss came in. "Well, he's off," she said, conspiratorial, jubilant. "Went the old forest road. Says he'll cut down to the Middle Valley way, along past Oak Springs, tomorrow."

"Good," said Tenar.

Bolder than usual, Moss sat down uninvited. "I gave him a loaf and a bit of cheese for the way."

"Thank you, Moss. That was kind."

"Mistress Goha." Moss's voice in the darkness took on the singsong resonance of her chanting and spellcasting. "There's a thing I was wanting to say to you, dearie, without going beyond what I can know, for I know you've lived among great folks and been one of 'em yourself, and that seals my mouth when I think of it. And yet there's things I know that you've had no way of knowing, for all the learning of the runes, and the Old Speech, and all you've learned from the wise, and in the foreign lands."

"That's so, Moss."

"Aye, well, then. So when we talked about how witch knows witch, and power knows power, and I said—of him who's gone now—that he was no mage now, whatever he had been, and still you would deny it—But I was right, wasn't I?"

"Yes."

"Aye. I was."

"He said so himself."

"O' course he did. He don't lie nor say this is that and that's this till you don't know which end's up, I'll say that for him. He's not one tries to drive the cart without the ox, either. But I'll say flat out I'm glad he's gone, for it wouldn't do, it wouldn't do any longer, being a different matter with him now, and all."

Tenar had no idea what she was talking about, except for her image of trying to drive the cart without the ox. "I don't know why he's so afraid," she said. "Well, I know in part, but I don't understand it, why he feels such shame. But I know he thinks that he should have died. And I know that all I understand about living is having your work to do, and being able to do it. That's the pleasure, and the glory, and all. And if you can't do the work, or it's taken from you, then what's any good? You have to have something. . . ."

Moss listened and nodded as at words of wisdom,

but after a slight pause she said, "It's a queer thing for an old man to be a boy of fifteen, no doubt!"

Tenar almost said, "What are you talking about, Moss?"—but something prevented her. She realized that she had been listening for Ged to come into the house from his roaming on the mountainside, that she was listening for the sound of his voice, that her body denied his absence. She glanced suddenly over at the witch, a shapeless lump of black perched on Ogion's chair by the empty hearth.

"Ah!" she said, a great many thoughts suddenly coming into her mind all at once.

"*That's* why," she said. "*That's* why I never—"

After a quite long silence, she said, "Do they—do wizards—is it a spell?"

"Surely, surely, dearie," said Moss. "They witch 'emselves. Some'll tell you they make a trade-off, like a marriage turned backward, with vows and all, and so get their power then. But to me that's got a wrong sound to it, like a dealing with the Old Powers more than what a true witch deals with. And the old mage, he told me they did no such thing. Though I've known some woman witches do it, and come to no great harm by it."

"The ones who brought me up did that, promising virginity."

"Oh, aye, no men, you told me, and them yurnix. Terrible!

"But why, but why—why did I never *think*—"

The witch laughed aloud. "Because that's the

power of 'em, dearie. You don't think! You can't! And nor do they, once they've set their spell. How could they? Given their power? It wouldn't do, would it, it wouldn't do. You don't get without you give as much. That's true for all, surely. So they know that, the witch men, the men of power, they know that better than any. But then, you know, it's an uneasy thing for a man not to be a man, no matter if he can call the sun down from the sky. And so they put it right out of mind, with their spells of binding. And truly so. Even in these bad times we've been having, with the spells going wrong and all, I haven't yet heard of a wizard breaking those spells, seeking to use his power for his body's lust. Even the worst would fear to. O' course, there's those will work illusions, but they only fool 'emselves. And there's witch men of little account, witch-tinkers and the like, some of them'll try their own spells of beguilement on country women, but for all I can see, those spells don't amount to much. What it is, is the one power's as great as the other, and each goes its own way. That's how I see it."

Tenar sat thinking, absorbed. At last she said, "They set themselves apart."

"Aye. A wizard has to do that."

"But you don't."

"Me? I'm only an old witchwoman, dearie."

"How old?"

After a minute Moss's voice in the darkness said, with a hint of laughter in it, "Old enough to keep out of trouble."

"But you said . . . You haven't been celibate."

"What's that, dearie?"

"Like the wizards."

"Oh, no. No, no! Never was anything to look at, but there was a way I could look at them . . . not witching, you know, dearie, you know what I mean . . . there's a way to look, and he'd come round, sure as a crow will caw, in a day or two or three he'd come around my place—'I need a cure for my dog's mange,' 'I need a tea for my sick granny,'—but I knew what it was they needed, and if I liked 'em well enough maybe they got it. And for love, for love—I'm not one o' them, you know, though maybe some witches are, but they dishonor the art, I say. I do my art for pay but I take my pleasure for love, that's what I say. Not that it's all pleasure, all that. I was crazy for a man here for a long time, years, a good-looking man he was, but a hard, cold heart. He's long dead. Father to that Townsend who's come back here to live, you know him. Oh, I was so heartset on that man I did use my art, I spent many a charm on him, but 'twas all wasted. All for nothing. No blood in a turnip. . . . And I came up here to Re Albi in the first place when I was a girl because I was in trouble with a man in Gont Port. But I can't talk of that, for they were rich, great folks. 'Twas they had the power, not I! They didn't want their son tangled with a common girl like me, foul slut they called me, and they'd have had me put out of the way, like killing a cat, if

I hadn't run off up here. But oh, I did like that lad, with his round, smooth arms and legs and his big, dark eyes, I can see him plain as plain after all these years. . . ."

They sat a long while silent in the darkness.

"When you had a man, Moss, did you have to give up your power?"

"Not a bit of it," the witch said, complacent.

"But you said you don't get unless you give. Is it different, then, for men and for women?"

"What isn't, dearie?"

"I don't know," Tenar said. "It seems to me we make up most of the differences, and then complain about 'em. I don't see why the Art Magic, why power, should be different for a man witch and a woman witch. Unless the power *itself* is different. Or the art."

"A man gives out, dearie. A woman takes in."

Tenar sat silent but unsatisfied.

"Ours is only a little power, seems like, next to theirs," Moss said. "But it goes down deep. It's all roots. It's like an old blackberry thicket. And a wizard's power's like a fir tree, maybe, great and tall and grand, but it'll blow right down in a storm. Nothing kills a blackberry bramble." She gave her hen-chuckle, pleased with her comparison. "Well, then!" she said briskly. "So as I said, it's maybe just as well he's on his way and out o' the way, lest people in the town begin to talk."

"To talk?"

"You're a respectable woman, dearie, and her reputation is a woman's wealth."

"Her wealth," Tenar repeated in the same blank way; then she said it again: "Her wealth. Her treasure. Her hoard. Her value. . . ." She stood up, unable to sit still, stretching her back and arms. "Like the dragons who found caves, who built fortresses for their treasure, for their hoard, to be safe, to sleep on their treasure, to be their treasure. Take in, take in, and never give out!"

"You'll know the value of a good reputation," Moss said drily, "when you've lost it. 'Tisn't everything. But it's hard to fill the place of."

"Would you give up being a witch to be respectable, Moss?"

"I don't know," Moss said after a while, thoughtfully. "I don't know as I'd know how. I have the one gift, maybe, but not the other."

Tenar went to her and took her hands. Surprised at the gesture, Moss got up, drawing away a little; but Tenar drew her forward and kissed her cheek.

The older woman put up one hand and timidly touched Tenar's hair, one caress, as Ogion had used to do. Then she pulled away and muttered about having to go home, and started to leave, and asked at the door, "Or would you rather I stayed, with them foreigners about?"

"Go on," Tenar said. "I'm used to foreigners."

❧ ❧ ❧ ❧

That night as she lay going to sleep she entered again into the vast gulfs of wind and light, but the light was smoky, red and orange-red and amber, as if the air itself were fire. In this element she was and was not; flying on the wind and being the wind, the blowing of the wind, the force that went free; and no voice called to her.

In the morning she sat on the doorstep brushing out her hair. She was not fair to blondness, like many Kargish people; her skin was pale, but her hair dark. It was still dark, hardly a thread of grey in it. She had washed it, using some of the water that was heating to wash clothes in, for she had decided the laundry would be her day's work, Ged being gone, and her respectability secure. She dried her hair in the sun, brushing it. In the hot, windy morning, sparks followed the brush and crackled from the flying ends of her hair.

Therru came to stand behind her, watching. Tenar turned and saw her so intent she was almost trembling.

"What is it, birdlet?"

"The fire flying out," the child said, with fear or exultation. "All over the sky!"

"It's just the sparks from my hair," Tenar said, a little taken aback. Therru was smiling, and she did not know if she had ever seen the child smile before. Therru reached out both her hands, the whole one and the burned, as if to touch and follow the flight of something around Tenar's loose, floating hair. "The fires, all flying out," she repeated, and she laughed.

At that moment Tenar first asked herself how Therru saw her—saw the world—and knew she did not know: that she could not know what one saw with an eye that had been burned away. And Ogion's words, *They will fear her*, returned to her; but she felt no fear of the child. Instead, she brushed her hair again, vigorously, so the sparks would fly, and once again she heard the little husky laugh of delight.

She washed the sheets, the dishcloths, her shifts and spare dress, and Therru's dresses, and laid them out (after making sure the goats were in the fenced pasture) in the meadow to dry on the dry grass, weighting down the things with stones, for the wind was gusty, with a late-summer wildness in it.

Therru had been growing. She was still very small and thin for her age, which must be about eight, but in the last couple of months, with her injuries healed at last and free of pain, she had begun to run about more and to eat more. She was fast outgrowing her clothes, hand-me-downs from Lark's youngest, a girl of five.

Tenar thought she might walk into the village and visit with Weaver Fan and see if he might have an end or two of cloth to give in exchange for the swill she had been sending for his pigs. She would like to sew something for Therru. And she would like to visit with old Fan, too. Ogion's death and

Ged's illness had kept her from the village and the people she had known there. They had pulled her away, as ever, from what she knew, what she knew how to do, the world she had chosen to live in—a world not of kings and queens, great powers and dominions, high arts and journeys and adventures (she thought as she made sure Therru was with Heather, and set off into town), but of common people doing common things, such as marrying, and bringing up children, and farming, and sewing, and doing the wash. She thought this with a kind of vengefulness, as if she were thinking it at Ged, now no doubt halfway to Middle Valley. She imagined him on the road, near the dell where she and Therru had slept. She imagined the slight, ashen-haired man going along alone and silently, with half a loaf of the witch's bread in his pocket, and a load of misery in his heart.

"It's time you found out, maybe," she thought to him. "Time you learned that you didn't learn everything on Roke!" As she harangued him thus in her mind, another image came into it: she saw near Ged one of the men who had stood waiting for her and Therru on that road. Involuntarily she said, "Ged, be careful!"—fearing for him, for he did not carry even a stick. It was not the big fellow with hairy lips that she saw, but another of them, a youngish man with a leather cap, the one who had stared hard at Therru.

She looked up to see the little cottage next to

Fan's house, where she had lived when she lived here. Between it and her a man was passing. It was the man she had been remembering, imagining, the man with a leather cap. He was going past the cottage, past the weaver's house; he had not seen her. She watched him walk on up the village street without stopping. He was going either to the turning of the hill road or to the mansion house.

Without pausing to think why, Tenar followed him at a distance until she saw which turn he took. He went on up the hill to the domain of the Lord of Re Albi, not down the road that Ged had gone.

She turned back then, and made her visit to old Fan.

Though almost a recluse, like many weavers, Fan had been kind in his shy way to the Kargish girl, and vigilant. How many people, she thought, had protected her respectability! Now nearly blind, Fan had an apprentice who did most of the weaving. He was glad to have a visitor. He sat as if in state in an old carved chair under the object from which his use-name came: a very large painted fan, the treasure of his family—the gift, so the story went, of a generous sea-pirate to his grandfather for some speedy sailmaking in time of need. It was displayed open on the wall. The delicately painted men and women in their gorgeous robes of rose and jade and azure, the towers and bridges and banners of Havnor Great Port, were all familiar to Tenar as soon as she saw the fan again. Visitors to Re Albi were often brought to see it. It was the finest thing, all agreed, in the village.

She admired it, knowing it would please the old man, and because it was indeed very beautiful, and he said, "You've not seen much to equal that, in all your travels, eh?"

"No, no. Nothing like it in Middle Valley at all," said she.

"When you was here, in my cottage, did I ever show you the other side of it?"

"The other side? No," she said, and nothing would do then but he must get the fan down; only she had to climb up and do it, carefully untacking it, since he could not see well enough and could not climb up on the chair. He directed her anxiously. She laid it in his hands, and he peered with his dim eyes at it, half closed it to make sure the ribs played freely, then closed it all the way, turned it over, and handed it to her.

"Open it slow," he said.

She did so. Dragons moved as the folds of the fan moved. Painted faint and fine on the yellowed silk, dragons of pale red, blue, green moved and grouped, as the figures on the other side were grouped, among clouds and mountain peaks.

"Hold it up to the light," said old Fan.

She did so, and saw the two sides, the two paintings, made one by the light flowing through the silk, so that the clouds and peaks were the towers of the city, and the men and women were winged, and the dragons looked with human eyes.

"You see?"

"I see," she murmured.

"I can't, now, but it's in my mind's eye. I don't show many that."

"It is very wonderful."

"I meant to show it to the old mage," Fan said, "but with one thing and another I never did."

Tenar turned the fan once more before the light, then remounted it as it had been, the dragons hidden in darkness, the men and women walking in the light of day.

Fan took her out next to see his pigs, a fine pair, fattening nicely towards autumn sausages. They discussed Heather's shortcomings as a swill-carrier. Tenar told him that she fancied a scrap of cloth for a child's dress, and he was delighted, pulling out a full width of fine linen sheeting for her, while the young woman who was his apprentice, and who seemed to have taken up his unsociability as well as his craft, clacked away at the broad loom, steady and scowling.

Walking home, Tenar thought of Therru sitting at that loom. It would be a decent living. The bulk of the work was dull, always the same over, but weaving was an honorable trade and in some hands a noble art. And people expected weavers to be a bit shy, often to be unmarried, shut away at their work as they were; yet they were respected. And working indoors at a loom, Therru would not have to show her face. But the claw hand? Could that hand throw the shuttle, warp the loom?

And was she to hide all her life?

But what was she to do? "Knowing what her life must be . . ."

Tenar set herself to think of something else. Of the dress she would make. Lark's daughter's dresses were coarse homespun, plain as mud. She could dye half this width, yellow maybe, or with red madder from the marsh; and then a full apron or overdress of white, with a ruffle to it. Was the child to be hidden at a loom in the dark and never have a ruffle to her skirt? And that would still leave enough for a shift, and a second apron if she cut out carefully.

"Therru!" she called as she approached the house. Heather and Therru had been in the broom-pasture when she left. She called again, wanting to show Therru the material and tell her about the dress. Heather came gawking around from the spring-house, hauling Sippy on a rope.

"Where's Therru?"

"With you," Heather replied so serenely that Tenar looked around for the child before she understood that Heather had no idea where she was and had simply stated what she wished to be true.

"Where did you leave her?"

Heather had no idea. She had never let Tenar down before; she had seemed to understand that Therru had to be kept more or less in sight, like a goat. But maybe it was Therru all along who had understood that, and had kept herself in sight? So Tenar thought, as having no comprehensible guidance from Heather, she began to look and call for the child, receiving no response.

She kept away from the cliff's edge as long as she could. Their first day there, she had explained to Therru that she must never go alone down the steep fields below the house or along the sheer edge north of it, because one-eyed vision cannot judge distance or depth with certainty. The child had obeyed. She always obeyed. But children forget. But she would not forget. But she might get close to the edge without knowing it. But surely she had gone to Moss's house. That was it—having been there alone, last night, she would go again. That was it, of course.

She was not there. Moss had not seen her.

"I'll find her, I'll find her, dearie," she assured Tenar; but instead of going up the forest path to look for her as Tenar had hoped she would, Moss began to knot up her hair in preparation for casting a spell of finding.

Tenar ran back to Ogion's house, calling again and again. And this time she looked down the steep fields below the house, hoping to see the little figure crouched playing among the boulders. But all she saw was the sea, wrinkled and dark, at the end of those falling fields, and she grew dizzy and sick-hearted.

She went to Ogion's grave and a short way past it up the forest path, calling. As she came back through the meadow, the kestrel was hunting in the same spot where Ged had watched it hunt. This time it stooped, and struck, and rose with some little creature in its talons. It flew fast to the forest. She's feeding her young, Tenar thought. All kinds of thoughts went through her mind very vivid and precise, as she passed the laundry laid out on the grass, dry now, she must take it up before evening. She must search around the house, the springhouse, the milking shed, more carefully. This was her fault. She had caused it to happen by thinking of making Therru into a weaver, shutting her away in the dark to work, to be respectable. When Ogion had said "Teach her, teach her all, Tenar!" When she knew that a wrong that cannot be repaired must be transcended. When she knew that the child had been given her and she had failed in her charge, failed her trust, lost her, lost the one great gift.

She went into the house, having searched every corner of the other buildings, and looked again in the alcove and round the other bed. She poured herself water, for her mouth was dry as sand.

Behind the door the three sticks of wood, Ogion's staff and the walking sticks, moved in the shadows, and one of them said, "Here."

The child was crouched in that dark corner, drawn into her own body so that she seemed no bigger than a little dog, head bent down to the shoulder, arms and legs pulled tight in, the one eye shut.

"Little bird, little sparrow, little flame, what is wrong? What happened? What have they done to you now?"

Tenar held the small body, closed and stiff as stone, rocking it in her arms. "How could you frighten me so? How could you hide from me? Oh, I was so angry!"

She wept, and her tears fell on the child's face.

"Oh Therru, Therru, Therru, don't hide away from me!"

A shudder went through the knotted limbs, and slowly they loosened. Therru moved, and all at once clung to Tenar, pushing her face into the hollow between Tenar's breast and shoulder, clinging tighter, till she was clutching desperately. She did not weep. She never wept; her tears had been burned out of her, maybe; she had none. But she made a long, moaning, sobbing sound.

Tenar held her, rocking her, rocking her. Very, very slowly the desperate grip relaxed. The head lay pillowed on Tenar's breast.

"Tell me," the woman murmured, and the child answered in her faint, hoarse whisper, "He came here."

Tenar's first thought was of Ged, and her mind, still moving with the quickness of fear, caught that, saw who "he" was to her, and gave it a wry grin in passing, but passed on, hunting, "Who came here?"

No answer but a kind of internal shuddering.

"A man," Tenar said quietly, "a man in a leather cap."

Therru nodded once.

"We saw him on the road, coming here."

No response.

"The four men—the ones I was angry at, do you remember? He was one of them."

But she recalled how Therru had held her head down, hiding the burned side, not looking up, as she had always done among strangers.

"Do you know him, Therru?"

"Yes."

"From—from when you lived in the camp by the river?"

One nod.

Tenar's arms tightened around her.

"He came here?" she said, and all the fear she had felt turned as she spoke into anger, a rage that burned in her the length of her body like a rod of fire. She gave a kind of laugh—"Hah!"—and remembered in that moment Kalessin, how Kalessin had laughed.

But it was not so simple for a human and a woman. The fire must be contained. And the child must be comforted.

"Did he see you?"

"I hid."

Presently Tenar said, stroking Therru's hair, "He will never touch you, Therru. Understand me and believe me: he will never touch you again. He'll never see you again unless I'm with you, and then he must deal with me. Do you understand, my dear, my precious, my beautiful? You need not fear him. You must not fear him. He wants you to fear him. He feeds on your fear. We will starve him, Therru. We'll starve him till he eats himself. Till he chokes gnawing on the bones of his own hands. . . . Ah, ah, ah, don't listen to me now, I'm only angry, only angry. . . . Am I red? Am I red like a Gontishwoman, now? Like a dragon, am I red?" She tried to joke; and Therru, lifting her head, looked up into her face from her own crumpled, tremulous, fire-eaten face and said, "Yes. You are a red dragon."

The idea of the man's coming to the house, being in the house, coming around to look at his handi-work, maybe thinking of improving on it, that idea whenever it recurred to Tenar came less as a thought than as a queasy fit, a need to vomit. But the nausea burned itself out against the anger.

They got up and washed, and Tenar decided that what she felt most of all just now was hunger. "I am hollow," she said to Therru, and set them out a sub-stantial meal of bread and cheese, cold beans in oil and herbs, a sliced onion, and dry sausage. Therru ate a good deal, and Tenar ate a great deal.

As they cleared up, she said, "For the present, Therru, I won't leave you at all, and you won't leave me. Right? And we should both go now to Aunty Moss's house. She was making a spell to find you, and she needn't bother to go on with it, but she might not know that."

Therru stopped moving. She glanced once at the open doorway, and shrank away from it.

"We need to bring in the laundry, too. On our way back. And when we're back, I'll show you the cloth I got today. For a dress. For a new dress, for you. A red dress."

The child stood, drawing in to herself.

"If we hide, Therru, we feed him. We will eat. And we will starve him. Come with me."

The difficulty, the barrier of that doorway to the outside was tremendous to Therru. She shrank from it, she hid her face, she trembled, stumbled, it was cruel to force her to cross it, cruel to drive her out of hiding, but Tenar was without pity. "Come!" she said, and the child came.

They walked hand-in-hand across the fields to Moss's house. Once or twice Therru managed to look up.

Moss was not surprised to see them, but she had a queer, wary look about her. She told Therru to run inside her house to see the ringneck hen's new chicks and choose which two might be hers; and Therru disappeared at once into that refuge.

"She was in the house all along," Tenar said. "Hiding."

"Well she might," said Moss.

"Why?" Tenar asked harshly. She was not in the hiding vein.

"There's—there's beings about," the witch said, not portentously but uneasily.

"There's scoundrels about!" said Tenar, and Moss looked at her and drew back a little.

"Eh, now," she said. "Eh, dearie. You have a fire around you, a shining of fire all about your head. I cast the spell to find the child, but it didn't go right. It went its own way somehow, and I don't know yet if it's ended. I'm bewildered. I saw great beings. I sought the little girl but I saw them, flying in the mountains, flying in the clouds. And now you have that about you, like your hair was afire. What's amiss, what's wrong?"

"A man in a leather cap," Tenar said. "A youngish man. Well enough looking. The shoulder seam of his vest's torn. Have you seen him round?"

Moss nodded. "They took him on for the haying at the mansion house."

"I told you that she"—Tenar glanced at the house—"was with a woman and two men? He's one of them."

"You mean, one of them that—"

"Yes."

Moss stood like a wood carving of an old woman, rigid, a block. "I don't know," she said at last. "I thought I knew enough. But I don't. What— What would— Would he come to—to *see* her?"

"If he's the father, maybe he's come to claim her."

"Claim her?"

"She's his property."

Tenar spoke evenly. She looked up at the heights of Gont Mountain as she spoke.

"But I think it's not the father. I think this is the other one. The one that came and told my friend in the village that the child had 'hurt herself.'"

Moss was still bewildered, still frightened by her own conjurations and visions, by Tenar's fierceness, by the presence of abominable evil. She shook her head, desolate. "I don't know," she said. "I thought I knew enough. How could he come back?"

"To eat," Tenar said. "To eat. I won't be leaving her alone again. But tomorrow, Moss, I might ask you to keep her here an hour or so, early in the day. Would you do that, while I go up to the manor house?"

"Aye, dearie. Of course. I could put a hiding spell on her, if you like. But . . . But they're up there, the great men from the King's City. . . ."

"Why, then, they can see how life is among the common folk," said Tenar, and Moss drew back again as if from a rush of sparks blown her way from a fire in the wind.

FINDING WORDS

THEY WERE MAKING HAY IN THE lord's long meadow, strung out across the slope in the bright shadows of morning. Three of the mowers were women, and of the two men one was a boy, as Tenar could make out from some distance, and the other was stooped and grizzled. She came up along the mown rows and asked one of the women about the man with the leather cap.

"Him from down by Valmouth, ah," said the mower. "Don't know where he's got to." The others came along the row, glad of a break. None of them knew where the man from Middle Valley was or why he wasn't mowing with them. "That kind don't stay," the grizzled man said. "Shiftless. You know him, miss's?"

"Not by choice," said Tenar. "He came lurking

about my place—frightened the child. I don't know what he's called, even."

"Calls himself Handy," the boy volunteered. The others looked at her or looked away and said nothing. They were beginning to piece out who she must be, the Kargish woman in the old mage's house. They were tenants of the Lord of Re Albi, suspicious of the villagers, leery of anything to do with Ogion. They whetted their scythes, turned away, strung out again, fell to work. Tenar walked down from the hillside field, past a row of walnut trees, to the road.

On it a man stood waiting. Her heart leapt. She strode on to meet him.

It was Aspen, the wizard of the mansion house. He stood gracefully leaning on his tall pine staff in the shade of a roadside tree. As she came out onto the road he said, "Are you looking for work?"

"No."

"My lord needs field hands. This hot weather's on the turn, the hay must be got in."

To Goha, Flint's widow, what he said was appropriate, and Goha answered him politely, "No doubt your skill can turn the rain from the fields till the hay's in." But he knew she was the woman to whom Ogion dying had spoken his true name, and, given that knowledge, what he said was so insulting and deliberately false as to serve as a clear warning. She had been about to ask him if he knew where the man Handy was. Instead, she said, "I came to say to the overseer here that a man he took on for the hay-making left my village as a thief and worse, not one he'd choose to have about the place. But it seems the man's moved on."

She gazed calmly at Aspen until he answered, with an effort, "I know nothing about these people."

She had thought him, on the morning of Ogion's death, to be a young man, a tall, handsome youth with a grey cloak and a silvery staff. He did not look as young as she had thought him, or he was young but somehow dried and withered. His stare and his voice were now openly contemptuous, and she answered him in Goha's voice: "To be sure. I beg your pardon." She wanted no trouble with him. She made to go on her way back to the village, but Aspen said, "Wait!"

She waited.

"'A thief and worse,' you say, but slander's cheap, and a woman's tongue worse than any thief. You come up here to make bad blood among the field hands, casting calumny and lies, the dragonseed every witch sows behind her. Did you think I did not know you for a witch? When I saw that foul imp that clings to you, do you think I did not know how it was begotten, and for what purposes? The man did well who tried to destroy that creature, but the job should be completed. You defied me once, across the body of the old wizard, and I forbore to punish you then, for his sake and in the presence of others. But now you've come too far, and I warn you, woman! I will not have you set foot on this domain. And if you cross my will or dare so much as speak to me again, I will have you driven from Re Albi, and off the Overfell, with the dogs at your heels. Have you understood me?"

"No," Tenar said. "I have never understood men like you."

She turned and set off down the road.

Something like a stroking touch went up her spine, and her hair lifted up on her head. She turned sharp round to see the wizard reach out his staff towards her, and the dark lightnings gather round it, and his lips part to speak. She thought in that moment, *Because Ged has lost his magery, I thought all men bad, but I was wrong!*—And a civil voice said, "Well, well. What have we here?"

Two of the men from Havnor had come out onto the road from the cherry orchards on the other side of it. They looked from Aspen to Tenar with bland and courtly expressions, as if regretting the necessity of preventing a wizard from laying a curse on a middle-aged widow, but really, really, it would not do.

"Mistress Goha," said the man with the gold-embroidered shirt, and bowed to her.

The other, the bright-eyed one, saluted her also, smiling. "Mistress Goha," he said, "is one who, like the King, bears her true name openly, I think, and unafraid. Living in Gont, she may prefer that we use her Gontish name. But knowing her deeds, I ask to do her honor; for she wore the Ring that no woman wore since Elfarran." He dropped to one knee as if it were the most natural thing in the world, took Tenar's right hand very lightly and quickly, and touched his forehead to her wrist. He released her and stood up, smiling that kind, collusive smile.

"Ah," said Tenar, flustered and warmed right through—"there's all kinds of power in the world!—Thank you."

The wizard stood motionless, staring. He had closed his mouth on the curse and drawn back his staff, but there was still a visible darkness about it and about his eyes.

She did not know whether he had known or had just now learned that she was Tenar of the Ring. It did not matter. He could not hate her more. To be a woman was her fault. Nothing could worsen or amend it, in his eyes; no punishment was enough. He had looked at what had been done to Therru, and approved.

"Sir," she said now to the older man, "anything less than honesty and openness seems dishonor to the king, for whom you speak—and act, as now. I'd like to honor the king, and his messengers. But my own honor lies in silence, until my friend releases me. I—I'm sure, my lords, that he'll send some word to you, in time. Only give him time, I pray you."

"Surely," said the one, and the other, "as much time as he wants. And your trust, my lady, honors us above all."

She went on down the road to Re Albi at last, shaken by the shock and change of things, the wizard's flaying hatred, her own angry contempt, her terror at the sudden knowledge of his will and power to do her harm, the sudden end of that terror in the refuge offered by the envoys of the king—the men who had come in the white-sailed ship from the haven itself, the Tower of the Sword and the Throne, the center of right and order. Her heart lifted up in gratitude. There was indeed a king upon that throne, and in his crown the chiefest jewel would be the Rune of Peace.

She liked the younger man's face, clever and kindly, and the way he had knelt to her as to a queen, and his smile that had a wink hidden in it. She turned to look back. The two envoys were walking up the road to the mansion house with the wizard Aspen. They seemed to be conversing with him amicably, as if nothing had happened.

That sank her surge of hopeful trust a bit. To be sure, they were courtiers. It wasn't their business to quarrel, or to judge and disapprove. And he was a wizard, and their host's wizard. Still, she thought, they needn't have walked and talked with him quite so comfortably.

❧ ❧ ❧ ❧

The men from Havnor stayed several days with the Lord of Re Albi, perhaps hoping that the archmage would change his mind and come to them, but they did not seek him, nor press Tenar about where he might be. When they left at last, Tenar told herself that she must make up her mind what to do. There was no real reason for her to stay here, and two strong reasons for leaving: Aspen and Handy, neither of whom could she trust to let her and Therru alone.

Yet she found it hard to make up her mind, because it was hard to think of going. In leaving Re Albi now she left Ogion, lost him, as she had not lost him while she kept his house and weeded his onions. And she thought, "I will never dream of the sky, down there." Here, where Kalessin had come, she was Tenar, she thought. Down in Middle Valley she would only be Goha again. She delayed. She said to herself, "Am I to fear those scoundrels, to run from them? That's what they want me to do. Are they to make me come and go at their will?" She said to herself, "I'll just finish the cheese-making." She kept Therru always with her. And the days went by.

Moss came with a tale to tell. Tenar had asked her about the wizard Aspen, not telling her the whole story but saying that he had threatened her— which, in fact, might well be all he had meant to do. Moss usually kept clear of the old lord's domain, but she was curious about what went on there, and not unwilling to find the chance to chat with some acquaintances there, a woman from whom she had learned midwifery and others whom she had attended as healer or finder. She got them talking about the doings at the mansion house. They all hated Aspen and so were quite ready to talk about him, but their tales must be heard as half spite and fear. Still, there would be facts among the fancies. Moss herself attested that until Aspen came three years ago, the younger lord, the grandson, had been fit and well, though a shy, sullen man, "scared-like," she said. Then about the time the young lord's mother died, the old lord had sent to Roke for a wizard— "What for? With Lord Ogion not a mile away? And they're all witchfolk themselves in the mansion."

But Aspen had come. He had paid his respects and no more to Ogion, and always, Moss said, stayed up at the mansion. Since then, less and less had been seen of the grandson, and it was said now that he lay day and night in bed, "like a sick baby, all shriveled up," said one of the women who had been into the house on some errand. But the old lord, "a hundred years old, or near, or more," Moss insisted—she had no fear of numbers and no respect for them—the old lord was flourishing, "full of juice," they said. And one of the men, for they would have only men wait on them in the mansion, had told one of the women that the old lord had hired the wizard to make him live forever, and that the wizard was doing that, feeding him, the man said, off the grandson's life. And the man saw no harm in it, saying, "Who wouldn't want to live forever?"

"Well," Tenar said, taken aback. "That's an ugly story. Don't they talk about all this in the village?"

Moss shrugged. It was a matter of "Let be" again. The doings of the powerful were not to be judged by the powerless. And there was the dim, blind loyalty, the rootedness in place: the old man was *their* lord, Lord of Re Albi, nobody else's business what he did. . . . Moss evidently felt this herself. "Risky," she said, "bound to go wrong, such a trick," but she did not say it was wicked.

No sign of the man Handy had been seen up at the mansion. Longing to be sure that he had left the Overfell, Tenar asked an acquaintance or two in the village if they had seen such a man, but she got unwilling and equivocal replies. They wanted no part of her affairs. "Let be. . . ." Only old Fan treated her as a friend and fellow-villager. And that might be because his eyes were so dim he could not clearly see Therru.

She took the child with her now when she went into the village, or any distance at all from the house.

Therru did not find this bondage wearisome. She stayed close by Tenar as a much younger child would do, working with her or playing. Her play was with cat's cradle, basket making, and with a couple of bone figures that Tenar had found in a little grass bag on one of Ogion's shelves. There was an animal that might be a dog or a sheep, a figure that might be a woman or a man. To Tenar they had no sense of power or danger about them, and Moss said, "Just toys." To Therru they were a great magic. She moved them about in the patterns of some silent story for hours at a time; she did not speak as she played. Sometimes she built houses for the person and the animal, stone cairns, huts of mud and straw. They were always in her pocket in their grass bag. She was learning to spin; she could hold the distaff in the burned hand and twist the drop-spindle with the other. They had combed the goats regularly since they had been there, and by now had a good sackful of silky goathair to be spun.

"But I should be teaching her," Tenar thought, distressed. "Teach her *all*, Ogion said, and what am I teaching her? Cooking and spinning?" Then another part of her mind said in Goha's voice, "And are those not true arts, needful and noble? Is wisdom all words?"

Still she worried over the matter, and one afternoon while Therru was pulling the goathair to clean and loosen it and she was carding it, in the shade of the peach tree, she said, "Therru, maybe it's time you began to learn the true names of things. There is a language in which all things bear their true names, and deed and word are one. By speaking that tongue Segoy raised the islands from the deeps. It is the language dragons speak."

The child listened, silent.

Tenar laid down her carding combs and picked up a small stone from the ground. "In that tongue," she said, "this is *tolk*."

Therru watched what she did and repeated the word, *tolk*, but without voice, only forming it with her lips, which were drawn back a little on the right side by the scarring.

The stone lay on Tenar's palm, a stone.

They were both silent.

"Not yet," Tenar said. "That's not what I have to teach you now." She let the stone fall to the ground, and picked up her combs and a handful of cloudy grey wool Therru had prepared for carding. "Maybe when you have your true name, maybe that will be the time. Not now. Now, listen. Now is the time for stories, for you to begin to learn the stories. I can tell you stories of the Archipelago and of the Kargad Lands. I told you a story I learned from my friend Aihal the Silent. Now I'll tell you one I learned from my friend Lark when she told it to her children and mine. This is the story of Andaur and Avad. As long ago as forever, as far away as Selidor, there lived a man called Andaur, a woodcutter, who went up in the hills alone. One day, deep in the forest, he cut a great oak tree down. As it fell it cried out to him in a human voice. . . ."

It was a pleasant afternoon for them both.

But that night as she lay by the sleeping child,

Tenar could not sleep. She was restless, concerned with one petty anxiety after another—did I fasten the pasture gate, does my hand ache from carding or is it arthritis beginning, and so on. Then she became very uneasy, thinking she heard noises outside the house. Why haven't I got me a dog? she thought. Stupid, not to have a dog. A woman and child living alone ought to have a dog these days. But this is Ogion's house! Nobody would come here to do evil. But Ogion is dead, dead, buried at the roots of the tree at the forest's edge. And no one will come. Sparrowhawk's gone, run away. Not even Sparrowhawk anymore, a shadow man, no good to anyone, a dead man forced to be alive. And I have no strength, there's no good in me. I say the word of the Making and it dies in my mouth, it is meaningless. A stone. I am a woman, an old woman, weak, stupid. All I do is wrong. All I touch turns to ashes, shadow, stone. I am the creature of darkness, swollen with darkness. Only fire can cleanse me. Only fire can eat me, eat me away like—

She sat up and cried out aloud in her own language, "The curse be turned, and turn!"—and brought her right arm out and down, pointing straight to the closed door. Then leaping out of bed, she went to the door, flung it open, and said into the cloudy night, "You come too late, Aspen. I was eaten long ago. Go clean your own house!"

There was no answer, no sound, but a faint, sour, vile smell of burning—singed cloth or hair.

She shut the door, set Ogion's staff against it, and looked to see that Therru still slept. She did not sleep herself, that night.

In the morning she took Therru into the village to ask Fan if he would want the yarn they had been spinning. It was an excuse to get away from the house and to be for a little while among people. The old man said he would be glad to weave the yarn, and they talked for a few minutes, under the great painted fan, while the apprentice scowled and clacked away grimly at the loom. As Tenar and Therru left Fan's house, somebody dodged around the corner of the little cottage where she had lived. Something, wasps or bees, were stinging Tenar's neck and head, and there was a patter of rain all round, a thundershower, but there were no clouds— Stones. She saw the pebbles strike the ground. Therru had stopped, startled and puzzled, looking around. A couple of boys ran from behind the cottage, half hiding, half showing themselves, calling out to each other, laughing.

"Come along," Tenar said steadily, and they walked to Ogion's house.

Tenar was shaking, and the shaking got worse as they walked. She tried to conceal it from Therru, who looked troubled but not frightened, not having understood what had happened.

As soon as they entered the house, Tenar knew someone had been there while they were in the village.

It smelled of burned meat and hair. The coverlet of their bed had been disarranged.

When she tried to think what to do, she knew there was a spell on her. It had been laid waiting for her. She could not stop shaking, and her mind was confused, slow, unable to decide. She could not think. She had said the word, the true name of the stone, and it had been flung at her, in her face—in the face of evil, the hideous face— She had dared speak— She could not speak—

She thought, in her own language, *I cannot think in Hardic. I must not.*

She could think, in Kargish. Not quickly. It was as if she had to ask the girl Arha, who she had been long ago, to come out of the darkness and think for her. To help her. As she had helped her last night, turning the wizard's curse back on him. Arha had not known a great deal of what Tenar and Goha knew, but she had known how to curse, and how to live in the dark, and how to be silent.

It was hard to do that, to be silent. She wanted to cry out. She wanted to talk—to go to Moss and tell her what had happened, why she must go, to say good-bye at least. She tried to say to Heather, "The goats are yours now, Heather," and she managed to say that in Hardic, so that Heather would understand, but Heather did not understand. She stared and laughed. "Oh, they're Lord Ogion's goats!" she said.

"Then—you—" Tenar tried to say "go on keeping

them for him," but a deadly sickness came into her and she heard her voice saying shrilly, "fool, halfwit, imbecile, woman!" Heather stared and stopped laughing. Tenar covered her own mouth with her hand. She took Heather and turned her to look at the cheeses ripening in the milking shed, and pointed to them and to Heather, back and forth, until Heather nodded vaguely and laughed again because she was acting so queer.

Tenar nodded to Therru—come!—and went into the house, where the foul smell was stronger, making Therru cower.

Tenar fetched out their packs and their travel shoes. In her pack she put her spare dress and shifts, Therru's two old dresses and the half-made new one and the spare cloth; the spindle whorls she had carved for herself and Therru; and a little food and a clay bottle of water for the way. In Therru's pack went Therru's best baskets, the bone person and the bone animal in their grass bag, some feathers, a little maze-mat Moss had given her, and a bag of nuts and raisins.

She wanted to say, "Go water the peach tree," but dared not. She took the child out and showed her. Therru watered the tiny shoot carefully.

They swept and straightened up the house, working fast, in silence.

Tenar set a jug back on the shelf and saw on the other end of the shelf the three great books, Ogion's books.

Arha saw them and they were nothing to her, big leather boxes full of paper.

But Tenar stared at them and bit her knuckle, frowning with the effort to decide, to know what to do, and to know how to carry them. She could not carry them. But she must. They could not stay here in the desecrated house, the house where hatred had come in. They were his. Ogion's. Ged's. Hers. The knowledge. Teach her all! She emptied their wool and yarn from the sack she had meant to carry it in and put the books in, one atop the other, and tied the neck of the bag with a leather strap with a loop to hold it by. Then she said, "We must go now, Therru." She spoke in Kargish, but the child's name was the same, it was a Kargish word, flame, flaming; and she came, asking no questions, carrying her little hoard in the pack on her back.

They took up their walking sticks, the hazel shoot and the alder branch. They left Ogion's staff beside the door in the dark corner. They left the door of the house wide open to the wind from the sea.

An animal sense guided Tenar away from the fields and away from the hill road she had come by. She took a shortcut down the steep-falling pastures, holding Therru's hand, to the wagon road that zigzagged down to Gont Port. She knew that if she met Aspen she was lost, and thought he might be waiting for her on the way. But not, maybe, on this way.

After a mile or so of the descent she began to be able to think. What she thought first was that she had taken the right road. For the Hardic words were coming back to her, and after a while, the true words, so that she stooped and picked up a stone and held it in her hand, saying in her mind, *tolk*; and she put that stone in her pocket. She looked out into the vast levels of air and cloud and said in her mind, once, *Kalessin*. And her mind cleared, as that air was clear.

They came into a long cutting shadowed by high, grassy banks and outcrops of rock, where she was a little uneasy. As they came out onto the turn they saw the dark-blue bay below them, and coming into it between the Armed Cliffs a beautiful ship under full sail. Tenar had feared the last such ship, but not this one. She wanted to run down the road to meet it.

That she could not do. They went at Therru's pace. It was a better pace than it had been two months ago, and going downhill made it easy, too. But the ship ran to meet them. There was a magewind in her sails; she came across the bay like a flying swan. She was in port before Tenar and Therru were halfway down the next long turning of the road.

Towns of any size at all were very strange places to Tenar. She had not lived in them. She had seen the greatest city in Earthsea, Havnor, once, for a while; and she had sailed into Gont Port with Ged, years ago, but they had climbed on up the road to the Overfell without pausing in the streets. The only other town she knew was Valmouth, where her daughter lived, a sleepy, sunny little harbor town where a ship trading from the Andrades was a great event, and most of the conversation of the inhabitants concerned dried fish.

She and the child came into the streets of Gont Port when the sun was still well above the western sea. Therru had walked fifteen miles without complaint and without being worn out, though certainly she was very tired. Tenar was tired too, having not slept the night before, and having been much distressed; and also Ogion's books had been a heavy burden. Halfway down the road she had put them into the backpack, and the food and clothing into the woolsack, which was better, but not all that much better. So they came trudging among outlying houses to the landgate of the city, where the road, coming between two carved stone dragons, turned into a street. There a man, the guard of the gate, eyed them. Therru bent her burned face down towards the shoulder and hid her burned hand under the apron of her dress.

"Will you be going to a house in town, mistress?" the guard asked, peering at the child.

Tenar did not know what to say. She did not know there were guards at city gates. She had nothing to pay a tollkeeper or an innkeeper. She did not know a soul in Gont Port—except, she thought now, the wizard, the one who had come up to bury Ogion, what was he called? But she did not know what he was called. She stood there with her mouth open, like Heather.

"Go on, go on," the guard said, bored, and turned away.

She wanted to ask him where she would find the road south across the headlands, the coast road to Valmouth; but she dared not waken his interest again, lest he decide she was after all a vagrant or a witch or whatever he and the stone dragons were supposed to keep out of Gont Port. So they went on between the dragons—Therru looked up, a little, to see them—and tramped along on cobblestones, more and more amazed, bewildered, and abashed. It did not seem to Tenar that anybody or anything in the world had been kept out of Gont Port. It was all here. Tall houses of stone, wagons, drays, carts, cattle, donkeys, marketplaces, shops, crowds, people, people—the farther they went the more people there were. Therru clung to Tenar's hand, sidling, hiding her face with her hair. Tenar clung to Therru's hand.

She did not see how they could stay here, so the only thing to do was get started south and go till nightfall—all too soon now—hoping to camp in the woods. Tenar picked out a broad woman in a broad white apron who was closing the shutters of a shop, and crossed the street, resolved to ask her for the road south out of the city. The woman's firm, red face looked pleasant enough, but as Tenar was getting up her courage to speak to her, Therru clutched her hard as if trying to hide herself against her, and looking up she saw coming down the street towards her the man with the leather cap. He saw her at the same instant. He stopped.

Tenar seized Therru's arm and half dragged, half swung her round. "Come!" she said, and strode straight on past the man. Once she had put him behind her she walked faster, going downhill towards the flare and dark of the sunset water and the docks and quais at the foot of the steep street. Therru ran with her, gasping as she had gasped after she was burned.

Tall masts rocked against the red and yellow sky. The ship, sails furled, lay against the stone pier, beyond an oared galley.

Tenar looked back. The man was following them, close behind. He was not hurrying.

She ran out onto the pier, but after a way Therru stumbled and could not go on, unable to get her breath. Tenar picked her up, and the child held to her, hiding her face in Tenar's shoulder. But Tenar could scarcely move, thus laden. Her legs shook under her. She took a step, and another, and another. She came to the little wooden bridge they had laid from the pier to the ship's deck. She laid her hand on its rail.

A sailor on deck, a bald, wiry fellow, looked her over. "What's wrong, miss's?" he said.

"Is—Is the ship from Havnor?"

"From the King's City, sure."

"Let me aboard!"

"Well, I can't do that," the man said, grinning, but his eyes shifted; he was looking at the man who had come to stand beside Tenar.

"You don't have to run away," Handy said to her. "I don't mean you any harm. I don't want to hurt you. You don't understand. I was the one got help for her, wasn't I? I was really sorry, what happened. I want to help you with her." He put out his hand as if drawn irresistibly to touch Therru. Tenar could not move. She had promised Therru that he would never touch her again. She saw the hand touch the child's bare, flinching arm.

"What do you want with her?" said another voice. Another sailor had taken the place of the bald one: a young man. Tenar thought he was her son.

Handy was quick to speak. "She's got—she took my kid. My niece. It's mine. She witched it, she run off with it, see—"

She could not speak at all. The words were gone from her again, taken from her. The young sailor was not her son. His face was thin and stern, with clear eyes. Looking at him, she found the words: "Let me come aboard. Please!"

The young man held out his hand. She took it,

and he brought her across the gangway onto the deck of the ship.

"Wait there," he said to Handy, and to her, "Come with me."

But her legs would not hold her up. She sank down in a heap on the deck of the ship from Havnor, dropping the heavy sack but clinging to the child. "Don't let him take her, oh, don't let them have her, not again, not again, not again!"

THE DOLPHIN

SHE WOULD NOT LET GO THE CHILD, she would not give the child to them. They were all men aboard the ship. Only after a long time did she begin to be able to take into her mind what they said, what had been done, what was happening. When she understood who the young man was, the one she had thought was her son, it seemed as if she had understood it all along, only she had not been able to think it. She had not been able to think anything.

He had come back onto the ship from the docks and now stood talking to a grey-haired man, the ship's master by the look of him, near the gangplank. He glanced over at Tenar, whom they had let stay crouching with Therru in a corner of the deck between the railing and a great windlass. The long day's weariness had won out over Therru's fear; she was fast asleep, close against Tenar, with her little pack for a pillow and her cloak for a blanket.

Tenar got up slowly, and the young man came to her at once. She straightened her skirts and tried to smooth her hair back. "I am Tenar of Atuan," she said. He stood still. She said, "I think you are the king."

He was very young, younger than her son, Spark. He could hardly be twenty yet. But there was a look to him that was not young at all, something in his eyes that made her think: He has been through the fire.

"My name is Lebannen of Enlad, my lady," he said, and he was about to bow or even kneel to her. She caught his hands so that they stood there face to face. "Not to me," she said, "nor I to you!"

He laughed in surprise, and held her hands while he stared at her frankly. "How did you know I sought you? Were you coming to me, when that man—?"

"No, no. I was running away—from him—from—from ruffians— I was trying to go home, that's all."

"To Atuan?"

"Oh, no! To my farm. In Middle Valley. On Gont, here." She laughed too, a laugh with tears in it. The tears could be wept now, and would be wept. She let go the king's hands so that she could wipe her eyes.

"Where is it, Middle Valley?" he asked.

"South and east, around the headlands there. Valmouth is the port."

"We'll take you there," he said, with delight in being able to offer it, to do it.

She smiled and wiped her eyes, nodding acceptance.

"A glass of wine. Some food, some rest," he said, "and a bed for your child." The ship's master, listening discreetly, gave orders. The bald sailor she remembered from what seemed a long time ago came forward. He was going to pick up Therru. Tenar stood between him and the child. She could not let him touch her. "I'll carry her," she said, her voice strained high.

"There's the stairs there, miss's. I'll do it," said the sailor, and she knew he was kind, but she could not let him touch Therru.

"Let me," the young man, the king, said, and with a glance at her for permission, he knelt, gathered up the sleeping child, and carried her to the hatchway and carefully down the ladder-stairs. Tenar followed.

He laid her on a bunk in a tiny cabin, awkwardly, tenderly. He tucked the cloak around her. Tenar let him do so.

In a larger cabin that ran across the stern of the ship, with a long window looking out over the twilit bay, he asked her to sit at the oaken table. He took a tray from the sailor boy that brought it, poured out red wine in goblets of heavy glass, offered her fruit and cakes.

She tasted the wine.

"It's very good, but not the Dragon Year," she said.

He looked at her in unguarded surprise, like any boy.

"From Enlad, not the Andrades," he said meekly.

"It's very fine," she assured him, drinking again. She took a cake. It was shortbread, very rich, not sweet. The green and amber grapes were sweet and tart. The vivid tastes of the food and wine were like the ropes that moored the ship, they moored her to the world, to her mind again.

"I was very frightened," she said by way of apology. "I think I'll be myself again soon. Yesterday— no, today, this morning—there was a——a spell—" It was almost impossible to say the word, she stammered at it: "A c-curse—laid on me. It took my speech, and my wits, I think. And we ran from that, but we ran right to the man, the man who—" She looked up despairingly at the young man listening to her. His grave eyes let her say what must be said. "He was one of the people who crippled the child. He and her parents. They raped her and beat her and burned her; these things happen, my lord. These things happen to children. And he keeps following her, to get at her. And—"

She stopped herself, and drank wine, making herself taste its flavor.

"And so from him I ran to you. To the haven." She looked about at the low, carved beams of the cabin, the polished table, the silver tray, the thin, quiet face of the young man. His hair was dark and soft, his skin a clear bronze-red; he was dressed well and plainly, with no chain or ring or outward mark of authority. But he looked the way a king should look, she thought.

"I'm sorry I let the man go," he said. "But he can be found again. Who was it laid the spell on you?"

"A wizard." She would not say the name. She did not want to think about all that. She wanted them all behind her. No retribution, no pursuit. Leave them to their hatreds, put them behind her, forget.

Lebannen did not press, but he asked, "Will you be safe from these men on your farm?"

"I think so. If I hadn't been so tired, so confused by the—by the—so confused in my mind, so that I couldn't think, I wouldn't have been afraid of Handy. What could he have done? With all the people about, in the street? I shouldn't have run from him. But all I could feel was her fear. She's so little, all she can do is fear him. She'll have to learn not to fear him. I have to teach her that . . ." She was wandering. Thoughts came into her head in Kargish. Had she been talking in Kargish? He would think she was mad, an old mad woman babbling. She glanced up at him furtively. His dark eyes were not on her; he gazed at the flame of the glass lamp that hung low over the table, a little, still, clear flame. His face was too sad for a young man's face.

"You came to find him," she said. "The archmage. Sparrowhawk."

"Ged," he said, looking at her with a faint smile. "You, and he, and I go by our true names."

"You and I, yes. But he, only to you and me."

He nodded.

"He's in danger from envious men, men of ill will, and he has no—no defense, now. You know that?"

She could not bring herself to be plainer, but Lebannen said, "He told me that his power as a mage was gone. Spent in the act that saved me, and all of us. But it was hard to believe. I wanted not to believe him."

"I too. But it is so. And so he—" Again she hesitated. "He wants to be alone until his hurts are healed," she said at last, cautiously.

Lebannen said, "He and I were in the dark land, the dry land, together. We died together. Together we crossed the mountains there. You can come back across the mountains. There is a way. He knew it. But the name of the mountains is Pain. The stones . . . The stones cut, and the cuts are long to heal."

He looked down at his hands. She thought of Ged's hands, scored and gashed, clenched on their wounds. Holding the cuts close, closed.

Her own hand closed on the small stone in her pocket, the word she had picked up on the steep road.

"Why does he hide from me?" the young man cried in grief. Then, quietly, "I hoped indeed to see him. But if he doesn't wish it, that's the end of it, of course." She recognized the courtliness, the civility, the dignity of the messengers from Havnor, and appreciated it; she knew its worth. But she loved him for his grief.

"Surely he'll come to you. Only give him time. He was so badly hurt—everything taken from him— But when he spoke of you, when he said your name, oh, then I saw him for a moment as he was—as he will be again— All pride!"

"Pride?" Lebannen repeated, as if startled.

"Yes. Of course, pride. Who should be proud, if not he?"

"I always thought of him as— He was so patient," Lebannen said, and then laughed at the inadequacy of his description.

"Now he has no patience," she said, "and is hard on himself beyond all reason. There's nothing we can do for him, I think, except let him go his own way and find himself at the end of his tether, as they say on Gont. . . ." All at once she was at the end of her own tether, so weary she felt ill. "I think I must rest now," she said.

He rose at once. "Lady Tenar, you say you fled from one enemy and found another; but I came seeking a friend, and found another." She smiled at his wit and kindness. What a nice boy he is, she thought.

The ship was all astir when she woke: creaking and groaning of timbers, thud of running feet overhead, rattle of canvas, sailors' shouts. Therru was hard to waken and woke dull, perhaps feverish, though she was always so warm that Tenar found it hard to judge her fevers. Remorseful for having dragged the fragile child fifteen miles on foot and for all that had happened yesterday, Tenar tried to cheer her by telling her that they were in a ship, and that there was a real king on the ship, and that the little room they were in was the king's own room; that the ship was taking them home, to the farm, and Aunty Lark would be waiting for them at home, and maybe Sparrowhawk would be there too. Not even that roused Therru's interest. She was blank, inert, mute.

On her small, thin arm Tenar saw a mark—four fingers, red, like a brand, as from a bruising grip. But Handy had not gripped her, he had only touched her. Tenar had told her, had promised her that he would never touch her again. The promise had been broken. Her word meant nothing. What word meant anything, against deaf violence?

She bent down and kissed the marks on Therru's arm.

"I wish I'd had time to finish your red dress," she said. "The king would probably like to see it. But then, I suppose people don't wear their best clothes on a ship, even kings."

Therru sat on the bunk, her head bent down, and did not answer. Tenar brushed her hair. It was growing out thick at last, a silky black curtain over the burned parts of the scalp. "Are you hungry, birdlet? You didn't have any supper last night. Maybe the king will give us breakfast. He gave me cakes and grapes last night."

No response.

When Tenar said it was time to leave the room, she obeyed. Up on deck she stood with her head bent to her shoulder. She did not look up at the white sails full of the morning wind, nor at the sparkling water, nor back at Gont Mountain rearing its bulk and majesty of forest, cliff, and peak into the sky. She did not look up when Lebannen spoke to her.

"Therru," Tenar said softly, kneeling by her, "when a king speaks to you, you answer."

She was silent.

The expression of Lebannen's face as he looked at her was unreadable. A mask perhaps, a civil mask for revulsion, shock. But his dark eyes were steady. He touched the child's arm very lightly, saying, "It must be strange for you, to wake up in the middle of the sea."

She would eat only a little fruit. When Tenar asked her if she wanted to go back to the cabin, she nodded. Reluctant, Tenar left her curled up in the bunk and went back up on deck.

The ship was passing between the Armed Cliffs,

towering grim walls that seemed to lean above the sails. Bowmen on guard in little forts like mud-swallows' nests high on the cliffs looked down at them on deck, and the sailors yelled cheerfully up at them. "Way for the king!" they shouted, and the reply came down not much louder than the calling of swallows from the heights, "The king!"

Lebannen stood at the high prow with the ship's master and an elderly, lean, narrow-eyed man in the grey cloak of a mage of Roke Island. Ged had worn such a cloak, a clean, fine one, on the day he and she brought the Ring of Erreth-Akbe to the Tower of the Sword; an old one, stained and dirty and travelworn, had been all his blanket on the cold stone of the Tombs of Atuan, and on the dirt of the desert mountains when they had crossed those mountains together. She was thinking of that as the foam flew by the ship's sides and the high cliffs fell away behind.

When the ship was out past the last reefs and had begun to swing eastward, the three men came to her. Lebannen said, "My lady, this is the Master Windkey of Roke Island."

The mage bowed, looking at her with praise in his keen eyes, and curiosity also; a man who liked to know which way the wind blew, she thought.

"Now I needn't hope the fair weather will hold, but can count on it," she said to him.

"I'm only cargo on a day like this," said the mage. "Besides, with a sailor like Master

Serrathen handling the ship, who needs a weatherworker?"

We are so polite, she thought, all Ladies and Lords and Masters, all bows and compliments. She glanced at the young king. He was looking at her, smiling but reserved.

She felt as she had felt in Havnor as a girl: a barbarian, uncouth among their smoothnesses. But because she was not a girl now, she was not awed, but only wondered at how men ordered their world into this dance of masks, and how easily a woman might learn to dance it.

It would take them only the day, they told her, to sail to Valmouth. They would make port there by late afternoon, with this fair wind in the sails.

Still very weary from the long distress and strain of the day before, she was content to sit in the seat the bald sailor contrived for her out of a straw mattress and a piece of sailcloth, and watch the waves and the gulls, and see the outline of Gont Mountain, blue and dreamy in the noon light, changing as they skirted its steep shores only a mile or two out from land. She brought Therru up to be in the sunshine, and the child lay beside her, watching and dozing.

A sailor, a very dark man, toothless, came on bare feet with soles like hooves and hideously gnarled toes, and put something down on the canvas near Therru. "For the little girl," he said hoarsely, and went off at once, though not far off. He looked around hopefully now and then from his work to see if she liked his gift and then pretended he had not looked around. Therru would not touch the little cloth-wrapped packet. Tenar had to open it. It was an exquisite carving of a dolphin, in bone or ivory, the length of her thumb.

"It can live in your grass bag," Tenar said, "with the others, the bone people."

At that Therru came to life enough to fetch out her grass bag and put the dolphin in it. But Tenar had to go thank the humble giver. Therru would not look at him or speak. After a while she asked to go back to the cabin, and Tenar left her there with the bone person, the bone animal, and the dolphin for company.

It's so easy, she thought with rage, it's so easy for Handy to take the sunlight from her, take the ship and the king and her childhood from her, and it's so hard to give them back! A year I've spent trying to give them back to her, and with one touch he takes them and throws them away. And what good does it do him—what's his prize, his power? Is power that—an emptiness?

She joined the king and the mage at the ship's railing. The sun was well to the west now, and the ship drove through a glory of light that made her think of her dream of flying with the dragons.

"Lady Tenar," the king said, "I give you no message for our friend. It seems to me that to do so is to lay a burden on you, and also to encroach upon his freedom; and I don't want to do either. I am to be crowned within the month. If it were he that held the crown, my reign would begin as my heart desires. But whether he's there or not, he brought me to my kingdom. He made me king. I will not forget it."

"I know you will not forget it," she said gently. He was so intense, so serious, armored in the formality of his rank and yet vulnerable in his honesty, the purity of his will. Her heart yearned to him. He thought he had learned pain, but he would learn it again and again, all his life, and forget none of it.

And therefore he would not, like Handy, do the easy thing to do.

"I'll bear a message willingly," she said. "It's no burden. Whether he'd hear it is up to him."

The Master Windkey grinned. "It always was," he said. "Whatever he did was up to him."

"You've known him a long time?"

"Even longer than you, my lady. Taught him," said the mage. "What I could. . . . He came to the School on Roke, you know, as a boy, with a letter from Ogion telling us that he had great power. But the first time I had him out in a boat, to learn how to speak to the wind, you know, he raised up a waterspout. I saw then what we were in for. I thought, Either he'll be drowned before he's sixteen, or he'll be archmage before he's forty. . . . Or I like to think I thought it."

"Is he still archmage?" Tenar asked. The question

seemed baldly ignorant, and when it was greeted by a silence, she feared it had been worse than ignorant.

The mage said finally, "There is now no Archmage of Roke." His tone was exceedingly cautious and precise.

She dared not ask what he meant.

"I think," said the king, "that the Healer of the Rune of Peace may be part of any council of this realm; don't you think so, sir?"

After another pause and evidently with a little struggle, the mage said, "Certainly."

The king waited, but he said no more.

Lebannen looked out at the bright water and spoke as if he began a tale: "When he and I came to Roke from the farthest west, borne by the dragon . . . " He paused, and the dragon's name spoke itself in Tenar's mind, *Kalessin*, like a struck gong.

"The dragon left me there, but bore him away. The keeper of the door of the House of Roke said then, 'He has done with doing. He goes home.' And before that—on the beach of Selidor—he bade me leave his staff, saying he was no mage now. So the Masters of Roke took counsel to choose a new archmage.

"They took me among them, that I might learn what it might be well for a king to know about the Council of the Wise. And also I was one of them to replace one of their number: Thorion, the Summoner, whose art was turned against him by that great evil which my lord Sparrowhawk found and ended. When we were there, in the dry land, between the wall and the mountains, I saw Thorion. My lord spoke to him, telling him the way back to life across the wall. But he did not take it. He did not come back."

The young man's strong, fine hands held hard to the ship's rail. He still gazed at the sea as he spoke. He was silent for a minute and then took up his story.

"So I made out the number, nine, who meet to choose the new archmage.

"They are . . . they are wise men," he said, with a glance at Tenar. "Not only learned in their art, but knowledgeable men. They use their differences, as I had seen before, to make their decision strong. But this time . . ."

"The fact is," said the master windkey, seeing Lebannen unwilling to seem to criticize the Masters of Roke, "we were all difference and no decision. We could come to no agreement. Because the archmage wasn't dead—was alive, you see, and yet no mage—and yet still a dragonlord, it seemed. . . . And because our Changer was still shaken from the turning of his own art on him, and believed that the Summoner would return from death, and begged us to wait for him. . . . And because the Master Patterner would not speak at all. He is a Karg, my lady, like yourself; did you know that? He came to us from Karego-At." His keen eyes watched her: which way does the wind blow? "So because of all that, we found ourselves at a loss. When the Doorkeeper asked for the names of those from whom we would choose, not a name was spoken. Everybody looked at everybody else. . . ."

"I looked at the ground," Lebannen said.

"So at last we looked to the one who knows the names: the Master Namer. And he was watching the Patterner, who hadn't said a word, but sat there among his trees like a stump. It's in the Grove we meet, you know, among those trees whose roots are deeper than the islands. It was late in the evening by then. Sometimes there's a light among those trees, but not that night. It was dark, no starlight, a cloudy sky above the leaves. And the Patterner stood up and spoke then—but in his own language, not in the Old Speech, nor in Hardic, but in Kargish. Few of us knew it or even knew what tongue it was, and we didn't know what to think. But the Namer told us what the Patterner had said. He said: *A woman on Gont*."

He stopped. He was no longer looking at her. After a bit she said, "Nothing more?"

"Not a word more. When we pressed him, he stared at us and couldn't answer; for he'd been in the vision, you see—he'd been seeing the shape of things, the pattern; and it's little of that can ever be put in words, and less into ideas. He knew no more what to think of what he'd said than the rest of us. But it was all we had."

The Masters of Roke were teachers, after all, and the Windkey was a very good teacher; he couldn't help but make his story clear. Clearer perhaps than he wanted. He glanced once again at Tenar, and away.

"So, you see, it seemed we should come to Gont. But for what? Seeking whom? 'A woman'—not much to go on! Evidently this woman is to guide us, show us the way, somehow, to our archmage. And at once, as you may think, my lady, you were spoken of—for what other woman on Gont had we ever heard of? It is no great island, but yours is a great fame. Then one of us said, 'She would lead us to Ogion.' But we all knew that Ogion had long ago refused to be archmage, and surely would not accept now that he was old and ill. And indeed Ogion was dying as we spoke, I think. Then another said, 'But she'd lead us also to Sparrowhawk!' And then we were truly in the dark."

"Truly," Lebannen said. "For it began to rain, there among the trees." He smiled. "I had thought I'd never hear rain fall again. It was a great joy to me."

"Nine of us wet," said the Windkey, "and one of us happy."

Tenar laughed. She could not help but like the man. If he was so wary of her, it behooved her to be wary of him; but to Lebannen, and in Lebannen's presence, only candor would do.

"Your 'woman on Gont' can't be me, then, for I

will not lead you to Sparrowhawk."

"It was my opinion," the mage said with apparent and perhaps real candor of his own, "that it couldn't be you, my lady. For one thing, he would have said your name, surely, in the vision. Very few are those who bear their true names openly! But I am charged by the Council of Roke to ask you if you know of any woman on this isle who might be the one we seek—sister or mother to a man of power, or even his teacher; for there are witches very wise in their way. Maybe Ogion knew such a woman? They say he knew every soul on this island, for all he lived alone and wandered in the wilderness. I wish he were alive to aid us now!"

She had thought already of the fisherwoman of Ogion's story. But that woman had been old when Ogion knew her, years ago, and must be dead by now. Though dragons, she thought, lived very long lives, it was said.

She said nothing for a while, and then only, "I know no one of that sort."

She could feel the mage's controlled impatience with her. What's she holding out for? What is it she wants? he was thinking, no doubt. And she wondered why it was she could not tell him. His deafness silenced her. She could not even tell him he was deaf.

"So," she said at last, "there is no archmage of Earthsea. But there is a king."

"In whom our hope and trust are well founded," the mage said with a warmth that became him well.

Lebannen, watching and listening, smiled.

"In these past years," Tenar said, hesitant, "there have been many troubles, many miseries. My—the little girl—Such things have been all too common. And I have heard men and women of power speak of the waning, or the changing, of their power."

"That one whom the archmage and my lord defeated in the dry land, that Cob, caused untold harm and ruin. We shall be repairing our art, healing our wizards and our wizardry, for a long time yet," the mage said, decisively.

"I wonder if there might be more to be done than repairing and healing," she said, "though that too, of course—But I wonder, could it be that . . . that one such as Cob could have such power because things were already altering . . . and that a change, a great change, has been taking place, has taken place? And that it's because of that change that we have a king again in Earthsea—perhaps a king rather than an archmage?"

The Windkey looked at her as if he saw a very distant storm cloud on the uttermost horizon. He even raised his right hand in the hint, the first sketch, of a windbinding spell, and then lowered it again. He smiled. "Don't be afraid, my lady," he said. "Roke, and the Art Magic, will endure. Our treasure is well guarded!"

"Tell Kalessin that," she said, suddenly unable to endure the utter unconsciousness of his disrespect. It made him stare, of course. He heard the dragon's name. But it did not make him hear her. How could he, who had never listened to a woman since his mother sang him his last cradle song, hear her?

"Indeed," said Lebannen, "Kalessin came to Roke, which is said to be defended utterly from dragons; and not through any spell of my lord's, for he had no magery then. . . . But I don't think, Master Windkey, that Lady Tenar was afraid for herself."

The mage made an earnest effort to amend his offense. "I'm sorry, my lady," he said, "I spoke as to an ordinary woman."

She almost laughed. She could have shaken him. She said only, indifferently, "My fears are ordinary fears." It was no use; he could not hear her.

But the young king was silent, listening.

A sailor boy up in the dizzy, swaying world of the masts and sails and rigging overhead called out clear and sweet, "Town there round the point!" And in a minute those down on deck saw the little huddle of slate roofs, the spires of blue smoke, a few glass windows catching the westering sun, and the docks and piers of Valmouth on its bay of satiny blue water.

"Shall I take her in or will you talk her in, my lord?" asked the calm ship's-master, and the Windkey replied, "Sail her in, master. I don't want to have to deal with all that flotsam!"—waving his hand at the dozens of fishing craft that littered the bay. So the king's ship, like a swan among ducklings, came tacking slowly in, hailed by every boat she passed.

Tenar looked along the docks, but there was no other seagoing vessel.

"I have a sailor son," she said to Lebannen. "I thought his ship might be in."

"What is his ship?"

He was third mate aboard the *Gull of Eskel,* but that was more than two years ago. He may have changed ships. He's a restless man." She smiled. "When I first saw you, I thought you were my son. You're nothing alike, only in being tall, and thin, and young. And I was confused, frightened. . . . Ordinary fears."

The mage had gone up on the master's station in the prow, and she and Lebannen stood alone.

"There is too much ordinary fear," he said.

It was her only chance to speak to him alone, and the words came out hurried and uncertain—"I wanted to say—but there was no use—but couldn't it be that there's a woman on Gont, I don't know who, I have no idea, but it could be that there is, or will be, or may be, a woman, and that they seek—that they need—her. Is it impossible?"

He listened. He was not deaf. But he frowned, intent, as if trying to understand a foreign language. And he said only, under his breath, "It may be."

A fisherwoman in her tiny dinghy bawled up, "Where from?" and the boy in the rigging called back like a crowing cock, "From the King's City!"

"What is this ship's name?" Tenar asked. "My son will ask what ship I sailed on."

"*Dolphin*," Lebannen answered, smiling at her. My son, my king, my dear boy, she thought. How I'd like to keep you nearby!

"I must go get my little one," she said.

"How will you get home?"

"Afoot. It's only a few miles up the valley." She pointed past the town, inland, where Middle Valley lay broad and sunlit between two arms of the mountain, like a lap. "The village is on the river, and my farm's a half mile from the village. It's a pretty corner of your kingdom."

"But will you be safe?"

"Oh, yes. I'll spend tonight with my daughter here in Valmouth. And in the village they're all to be depended on. I won't be alone."

Their eyes met for a moment, but neither spoke the name they both thought.

"Will they be coming again, from Roke?" she asked. Looking for the 'woman on Gont'—or for him?"

"Not for him. That, if they propose again, I will forbid," Lebannen said, not realizing how much he told her in those three words. "But as for their search for a new archmage, or for the woman of the Patterner's vision, yes, that may bring them here. And perhaps to you."

"They'll be welcome at Oak Farm," she said. "Though not as welcome as you would be."

"I will come when I can," he said, a little sternly; and a little wistfully, "if I can."

HOME

MOST OF THE PEOPLE OF VALMOUTH came down to the docks to see the ship from Havnor, when they heard that the king was aboard, the new king, the young king that the new songs were about. They didn't know the new songs yet, but they knew the old ones, and old Relli came with his harp and sang a piece of the *Deed of Morred*, for a king of Earthsea would be the heir of Morred for certain. Presently the king himself came on deck, as young and tall and handsome as could be, and with him a mage of Roke, and a woman and a little girl in old cloaks not much better than beggars, but he treated them as if they were a queen and a princess, so maybe that's what they were. "Maybe it's his mother," said Shinny, trying to see over the heads of the men in front of her, and then her friend

Apple clutched her arm and said in a kind of whispered shriek, "It is—it's mother!"

"Whose mother?" said Shinny, and Apple said, "Mine. And that's Therru." But she did not push forward in the crowd, even when an officer of the ship came ashore to invite old Relli aboard to play for the king. She waited with the others. She saw the king receive the notables of Valmouth, and heard Relli sing for him. She watched him bid his guests farewell, for the ship was going to stand out to sea again, people said, before night fell, and be on her way home to Havnor. The last to come across the gangplank were Therru and Tenar. To each the king gave the formal embrace, laying cheek to cheek, kneeling to embrace Therru. "Ah!" said the crowd on the dock. The sun was setting in a mist of gold, laying a great gold track across the bay, as the two came down the railed gangplank. Tenar lugged a heavy pack and bag; Therru's face was bent down and hidden by her hair. The gangplank was run in, and the sailors leapt to the rigging, and the officers shouted, and the ship *Dolphin* turned on her way. Then Apple made her way through the crowd at last.

"Hello, mother," she said, and Tenar said, "Hello, daughter." They kissed, and Apple picked up Therru and said, "How you've grown! You're twice the girl you were. Come on, come on home with me."

But Apple was a little shy with her mother, that evening, in the pleasant house of her young merchant husband. She gazed at her several times with a thoughtful, almost a wary look. "It never meant a thing to me, you know, mother," she said at the door of Tenar's bedroom—"all that—the Rune of Peace—and you bringing the Ring to Havnor. It was just like one of the songs. A thousand years ago! But it really was you, wasn't it?"

"It was a girl from Atuan," Tenar said. "A thousand years ago. I think I could sleep for a thousand years, just now."

"Go to bed, then." Apple turned away, then turned back, lamp in hand. "King-kisser," she said.

"Get along with you," said Tenar.

Apple and her husband kept Tenar a couple of days, but after that she was determined to go to the farm. So Apple walked with her and Therru up along the placid, silvery Kaheda. Summer was turning to autumn. The sun was still hot, but the wind was cool. The foliage of trees had a weary, dusty look to it, and the fields were cut or in harvest.

Apple spoke of how much stronger Therru was, and how sturdily she walked now.

"I wish you'd seen her at Re Albi," Tenar said, "before—" and stopped. She had decided not to worry her daughter with all that.

"What did happen?" Apple asked, so clearly resolved to know that Tenar gave in and answered in a low voice, "One of *them*."

Therru was a few yards ahead of them,

long-legged in her outgrown dress, hunting black-berries in the hedgerows as she walked.

"Her father?" Apple asked, sickened at the thought.

"Lark said the one that seems to be the father called himself Hake. This one's younger. He's the one that came to Lark to tell her. He's called Handy. He was . . . hanging around at Re Albi. And then by ill luck we ran into him in Gont Port. But the king sent him off. And now I'm here and he's there, and all that's done with."

"But Therru was frightened," Apple said, a bit grimly.

Tenar nodded.

"But why did you go to Gont Port?"

"Oh, well, this man Handy was working for a man . . . a wizard at the lord's house in Re Albi, who took a dislike to me. . . ." She tried to think of the wizard's use-name and could not; all she could think of was *Tuaho*, a Kargish word for a kind of tree, she could not remember what tree.

"So?"

"Well, so, it seemed better just to come on home."

"But what did this wizard dislike you for?"

"For being a woman, mostly."

"Bah," said Apple. "Old cheese rind."

"Young cheese rind, in this case."

"Worse yet. Well, nobody around here that I know of has seen the parents, if that's the word for 'em. But if they're still hanging about, I don't like your being alone in the farmhouse."

It is pleasant to be mothered by a daughter, and to behave as a daughter to one's daughter. Tenar said impatiently, "I'll be perfectly all right!"

"You could at least get a dog."

"I've thought of that. Somebody in the village might have a pup. We'll ask Lark when we stop by there."

"Not a puppy, mother. A dog."

"But a young one—one Therru could play with," she pleaded.

"A nice puppy that will come and kiss the burglars," said Apple, stepping along buxom and grey-eyed, laughing at her mother.

They came to the village about midday. Lark welcomed Tenar and Therru with a festivity of embraces, kisses, questions, and things to eat. Lark's quiet husband and other villagers stopped by to greet Tenar. She felt the happiness of homecoming.

Lark and the two youngest of her seven children, a boy and a girl, accompanied them out to the farm. The children had known Therru since Lark first brought her home, of course, and were used to her, though two months' separation made them shy at first. With them, even with Lark, she remained withdrawn, passive, as in the bad old days.

"She's worn out, confused by all this traveling. She'll get over it. She's come along wonderfully," Tenar said to Lark, but Apple would not let her get out of it so easily. "One of *them* turned up and terrified her and mother both," said Apple. And little by little, between them, the daughter and the friend got the story out of Tenar that afternoon, as they opened up the cold, stuffy, dusty house, put it to rights, aired the bedding, shook their heads over sprouted onions, laid in a bit of food in the pantry, and set a large kettle of soup on for supper. What they got came a word at a time. Tenar could not seem to tell them what the wizard had done; a spell, she said vaguely, or maybe it was that he had sent Handy after her. But when she came to talk about the king, the words came tumbling out.

"And then there he was—the king!—like a swordblade—And Handy shrinking and shrivelling back from him— And I thought he was Spark! I did, I really did for a moment, I was so—so beside myself—"

"Well," said Apple, "that's all right, because Shinny thought you were his mother. When we were on the docks watching you come sailing in in your glory. She kissed him, you know, Aunty Lark. Kissed the king—just like that. I thought next thing she'd kiss that mage. But she didn't."

"I should think not, what an idea. What mage?" said Lark, with her head in a cupboard. "Where's your flour bin, Goha?"

"Your hand's on it. A Roke mage, come looking for a new archmage."

"Here?"

"Why not?" said Apple. "The last one was from Gont, wasn't he? But they didn't spend much time looking. They sailed straight back to Havnor, once they'd got rid of mother."

"How you do talk."

"He was looking for a woman, he said," Tenar told them. "'A woman on Gont.' But he didn't seem too happy about it."

"A wizard looking for a woman? Well, that's something new," said Lark. "I'd have thought this'd be weevilly by now, but it's perfectly good. I'll bake up a bannock or two, shall I? Where's the oil?"

"I'll need to draw some from the crock in the cool-room. Oh, Shandy! There you are! How are you? How's Clearbrook? How's everything been? Did you sell the ram lambs?"

They sat down nine to supper. In the soft yellow light of the evening in the stone-floored kitchen, at the long farm table, Therru began to lift her head a little, and spoke a few times to the other children; but there was still a cowering in her, and as it grew darker outside she sat so that her seeing eye could watch the window.

Not until Lark and her children had gone home in the twilight, and Apple was singing Therru to sleep, and she was washing up the dishes with Shandy, did Tenar ask about Ged. Somehow she had not wanted to while Lark and Apple were listening; there would have been so many explanations. She had forgotten to mention his being at Re

Albi at all. And she did not want to talk about Re Albi any more. Her mind seemed to darken when she tried to think of it.

"Did a man come here last month from me—to help out with the work?"

"Oh, I clean forgot!" cried Shandy. "Hawk, you mean—him with the scars on his face?"

"Yes," Tenar said. "Hawk."

"Oh, aye, well, he'll be away up on Hot Springs Mountain, above Lissu, up there with the sheep, with Serry's sheep, I believe. He come here and says how you sent him, and there wasn't a lick o' work for him here, you know, with Clearbrook and me looking after the sheep and I been dairying and old Tiff and Sis helping me out when needed, and I racked my brains, but Clearbrook he says, 'Go ask Serry's man, Farmer Serry's overseer up by Kahedanan, do they need herders in the high pastures,' he said, and that Hawk went off and did that, and got took on, and was off next day. 'Go ask Serry's man,' Clearbrook told him, and that's what he done, and got took right on. So he'll be back down with the flocks come fall, no doubt. Up there on the Long Fells above Lissu, in the high pastures. I think maybe it was goats they wanted him for. Nice-spoken fellow. Sheep or goats, I don't remember which. I hope it's all right with you that we didn't keep him on here, Goha, but it's the truth there wasn't a lick o' work for him what with me and Clearbrook and old Tiff, and Sis got the flax in.

And he said he'd been a goatherd over there where he come from, away round the mountain, some place above Armouth he said, though he said he'd never herded sheep. Maybe it'll be goats they've got him with up there."

"Maybe," said Tenar. She was much relieved and much disappointed. She had wanted to know him safe and well, but she had wanted also to find him here.

But it was enough, she told herself, simply to be home—and maybe better that he was not here, that none of all that was here, all the griefs and dreams and wizardries and terrors of Re Albi left behind, for good. She was here, now, and this was home, these stone floors and walls, these small-paned windows, outside which the oaks stood dark in starlight, these quiet, orderly rooms. She lay awake awhile that night. Her daughter slept in the next room, the children's room, with Therru, and Tenar lay in her own bed, her husband's bed, alone.

She slept. She woke, remembering no dream.

After a few days at the farm she scarcely gave a thought to the summer passed on the Overfell. It was long ago and far away. Despite Shandy's insistence on there not being a lick o' work to be done about the farm, she found plenty that needed doing: all that had been left undone over the summer and all that had to be done in the season of harvest in the fields and dairy. She worked from daybreak till nightfall, and if by chance she had an hour to sit down, she spun, or sewed for Therru. The red dress was finished at last, and a pretty dress it was, with a white apron for fancy wear and an orangey-brown one for everyday. "Now, then, you look beautiful!" said Tenar in her seamstress's pride, when Therru first tried it on.

Therru turned her face away.

"You are beautiful," Tenar said in a different tone. "Listen to me, Therru. Come here. You have scars, ugly scars, because an ugly, evil thing was done to you. People see the scars. But they see you, too, and you aren't the scars. You aren't ugly. You aren't evil. You are Therru, and beautiful. You are Therru who can work, and walk, and run, and dance, beautifully, in a red dress."

The child listened, the soft, unhurt side of her face as expressionless as the rigid, scar-masked side.

She looked down at Tenar's hands, and presently touched them with her small fingers. "It is a beautiful dress," she said in her faint, hoarse voice.

When Tenar was alone, folding up the scraps of red material, tears came stinging into her eyes. She felt rebuked. She had done right to make the dress, and she had spoken the truth to the child. But it was not enough, the right and the truth. There was a gap, a void, a gulf, on beyond the right and the truth. Love, her love for Therru and Therru's for her, made a bridge across that gap, a bridge of spider web, but love did not fill or close it. Nothing did that. And the child knew it better than she.

The day of the equinox came, a bright sun of autumn burning through the mist. The first bronze was in the leaves of the oaks. As she scrubbed cream pans in the dairy with the window and door wide open to the sweet air, Tenar thought that her young king was being crowned this day in Havnor. The lords and ladies would walk in their clothes of blue and green and crimson, but he would wear white, she thought. He would climb up the steps to the Tower of the Sword, the steps she and Ged had climbed. The crown of Morred would be placed on his head. He would turn as the trumpets sounded and seat himself on the throne that had been empty so many years, and look at his kingdom with those dark eyes that knew what pain was, what fear was. "Rule well, rule long," she thought, "poor boy!" And she thought, "It should have been Ged there putting the crown on his head. He should have gone."

But Ged was herding the rich man's sheep, or maybe goats, up in the high pastures. It was a fair, dry, golden autumn, and they would not be bringing the flocks down till the snow fell up there on the heights.

When she went into the village, Tenar made a point of going by Ivy's cottage at the end of Mill Lane. Getting to know Moss at Re Albi had made her wish to know Ivy better, if she could once get past the witch's suspicion and jealousy. She missed

Moss, even though she had Lark here; she had learned from her and had come to love her, and Moss had given both her and Therru something they needed. She hoped to find a replacement of that here. But Ivy, though a great deal cleaner and more reliable than Moss, had no intention of giving up her dislike of Tenar. She treated her overtures of friendship with the contempt that, Tenar admitted, they perhaps deserved. "You go your way, I go mine," the witch told her in everything but words; and Tenar obeyed, though she continued to treat Ivy with marked respect when they met. She had, she thought, slighted her too often and too long, and owed her reparation. Evidently agreeing, the witch accepted her due with unbending ire.

In mid-autumn the sorcerer Beech came up the valley, called by a rich farmer to treat his gout. He stayed on awhile in the Middle Valley villages as he usually did, and passed one afternoon at Oak Farm, checking up on Therru and talking with Tenar. He wanted to know anything she would tell him of Ogion's last days. He was the pupil of a pupil of Ogion's and a devout admirer of the mage of Gont. Tenar found it was not so hard to talk about Ogion as about other people of Re Albi, and told him all she could. When she had done he asked a little cautiously, "And the archmage—did he come?"

"Yes," Tenar said.

Beech, a smooth-skinned, mild-looking man in his forties, tending a little to fat, with dark half-circles under his eyes that belied the blandness of his face, glanced at her, and asked nothing.

"He came after Ogion's death. And left," she said. And presently, "He's not archmage now. You knew that?"

Beech nodded.

"Is there any word of their choosing a new archmage?"

The sorcerer shook his head. "There was a ship in from the Enlades not long ago, but no word from her crew of anything but the coronation. They were full of that! And it sounds as if all auspices and events were fortunate. If the goodwill of mages is valuable, then this young king of ours is a rich man. . . . And an active one, it seems. There's an order come overland from Gont Port just before I left Valmouth, for the nobles and merchants and the mayor and his council to meet together and see to it that the bailiffs of the district be worthy and accountable men, for they're the king's officers now, and are to do his will and enact his law. Well, you can imagine how Lord Heno greeted that!" Heno was a notable patron of pirates, who had long kept most of the bailiffs and sea-sheriffs of South Gont in his pocket. "But there were men willing to face up to Heno, with the king standing behind them. They dismissed the old lot then and there, and named fifteen new bailiffs, decent men, paid out of the mayor's funds. Heno stormed off swearing destruction. It's a new day! Not all at once, of course, but it's coming. I wish Master Ogion had lived to see it."

"He did," Tenar said. "As he was dying, he smiled, and he said, 'All changed. . . .'"

Beech took this in his sober way, nodding slowly. "All changed," he repeated.

After a while he said, "The little one's doing very well."

"Well enough. . . . Sometimes I think not well enough."

"Mistress Goha," said the sorcerer, "if I or any sorcerer or witch or I daresay wizard had kept her, and used all the power of healing of the Art Magic for her all these months since she was injured, she wouldn't be better off. Maybe not as well as she is. You have done *all* that can be done, mistress. You have done a wonder."

She was touched by his earnest praise, and yet it made her sad; and she told him why. "It isn't enough," she said. "I can't heal her. She is . . . What is she to do? What will become of her?" She ran off the thread she had been spinning onto the spindle-shank, and said, "I am afraid."

"For her," Beech said, half querying.

"Afraid because her fear draws to it, to her, the cause of her fear. Afraid because—"

But she could not find the words for it.

"If she lives in fear, she will do harm," she said at last. "I'm afraid of that."

The sorcerer pondered. "I've thought," he said at

last in his diffident way, "that maybe, if she has the gift, as I think she does, she might be trained a bit in the Art. And, as a witch, her . . . appearance wouldn't be so much against her—possibly." He cleared his throat. "There are witches who do very creditable work," he said.

Tenar ran a little of the thread she had spun between her fingers, testing it for evenness and strength. "Ogion told me to teach her. 'Teach her all,' he said, and then, 'Not Roke.' I don't know what he meant."

Beech had no difficulty with it. "He meant that the learning of Roke—the High Arts—wouldn't be suitable for a girl," he explained. "Let alone one so handicapped. But if he said to teach her all but that lore, it would seem that he too saw her way might well be the witches' way." He pondered again, more cheerfully, having got the weight of Ogion's opinion on his side. "In a year or two, when she's quite strong, and grown a bit more, you might think of asking Ivy to begin teaching her a bit. Not too much, of course, even of that kind of thing, till she has her true name."

Tenar felt a strong, immediate resistance to the suggestion. She said nothing, but Beech was a sensitive man. "Ivy's dour," he said. "But what she knows, she does honestly. Which can't be said of all witches. *Weak as women's magic,* you know, and *wicked as women's magic!* But I've known witches with real healing power. Healing befits a woman. It comes natural to her. And the child might be drawn to that—having been so hurt herself."

His kindness was, Tenar thought, innocent.

She thanked him, saying that she would think carefully about what he had said. And indeed she did so.

Before the month was out, the villages of Middle Valley had met at the Round Barn of Sodeva to appoint their own bailiffs and officers of the peace and to levy a tax upon themselves to pay the bailiffs' wages with. Such were the king's orders, brought to the mayors and elders of the villages, and readily obeyed, for there were as many sturdy beggars and thieves on the roads as ever, and the villagers and farmers were eager to have order and safety. Some ugly rumors went about, such as that Lord Heno had formed a Council of Scoundrels and was enlisting all the blackguards in the countryside to go about in gangs breaking the heads of the king's bailies; but most people said, "Just let 'em try!" and went home telling each other that now an honest man could sleep safe abed at night, and what went wrong the king was setting right, though the taxes were beyond all reason and they'd all be poor men forever trying to pay them.

Tenar was glad to hear of all this from Lark, but did not pay it much heed. She was working very hard; and since she had got home she had, almost without being aware of it, resolved not to let the thought of Handy or any such ruffian rule her life or Therru's. She could not keep the child with her every moment, renewing her terrors, forever reminding her of what she could not remember and live. The child must be free and know herself to be free, to grow in grace.

She had gradually lost the shrinking, fearful manner, and by now went all about the farm and the byways and even into the village by herself. Tenar said no word of caution to her, even when she had to prevent herself from doing so. Therru was safe on the farm, safe in the village, no one was going to hurt her: that must be taken as unquestionable. And indeed Tenar did not often question it. With herself and Shandy and Clearbrook around the place, and Sis and Tiff down in the lower house, and Lark's family all over the village, in the sweet autumn of the Middle Valley, what harm was going to come to the child?

She'd get a dog, too, when she heard of one she wanted: one of the big grey Gontish sheep-guards, with their wise, curly heads.

Now and then she thought, as she had at Re Albi, "I must be teaching the child! Ogion said so." But somehow nothing seemed to get taught to her but farm work, and stories, in the evening, as the nights drew in and they began to sit by the kitchen fire after supper before they went to bed. Maybe Beech was right, and Therru should be sent to a witch to learn what witches knew. It was better than apprenticing her to a weaver, as Tenar had thought of doing. But not all that much better. And she was still not very big; and was very ignorant for her age, for she had been taught nothing before she came to Oak Farm. She had been like a little animal, barely knowing human speech, and no human skills. She learned quickly and was twice as obedient and diligent as Lark's unruly girls and laughing, lazy boys. She could clean and serve and spin, cook a little, sew a little, look after poultry, fetch the cows, and do excellent work in the dairy. A proper farm-lassie, old Tiff called her, fawning a bit. Tenar had also seen him make the sign to avert evil, surreptitiously, when Therru passed him. Like most people, Tiff believed that you are what happens to you. The rich and strong must have virtue; one to whom evil has been done must be bad, and may rightly be punished.

In which case it would not help much if Therru became the properest farm-lassie in Gont. Not even prosperity would diminish the visible brand of what had been done to her. So Beech had thought of her being a witch, accepting, making use, of the brand. Was that what Ogion had meant, when he said "Not Roke"—when he said "They will fear her"? Was that all?

One day when a managed chance brought them together in the village street, Tenar said to Ivy, "There's a question I want to ask you, Mistress Ivy. A matter of your profession."

The witch eyed her. She had a scathing eye.

"My profession, is it?"

Tenar nodded, steady.

"Come on, then," Ivy said with a shrug, leading off down Mill Lane to her little house.

It was not a den of infamy and chickens, like Moss's house, but it was a witch-house, the beams hung thick with dried and drying herbs, the fire banked under grey ash with one tiny coal winking like a red eye, a lithe, fat, black cat with one white mustache sleeping up on a shelf, and everywhere a profusion of little boxes, pots, ewers, trays, and stoppered bottles, all aromatic, pungent or sweet or strange.

"What can I do for you, Mistress Goha?" Ivy asked, very dry, when they were inside.

"Tell me, if you will, if you think my ward, Therru, has any gift for your art—any power in her."

"She? Of course!" said the witch.

Tenar was a bit floored by the prompt and contemptuous answer. "Well," she said. "Beech seemed to think so."

"A blind bat in a cave could see it," said Ivy. "Is that all?"

"No. I want your advice. When I've asked my question, you can tell me the price of the answer. Fair?"

"Fair."

"Should I prentice Therru for a witch, when she's a bit older?"

Ivy was silent for a minute, deciding on her fee, Tenar thought. Instead, she answered the question. "I would not take her," she said.

"Why?"

"I'd be afraid to," the witch answered, with a sudden fierce stare at Tenar.

"Afraid? Of what?"

"Of her! What is she?"

"A child. An ill-used child!"

"That's not all she is."

Dark anger came into Tenar and she said, "Must a prentice witch be a virgin, then?"

Ivy stared. She said after a moment, "I didn't mean that."

"What did you mean?"

"I mean I don't know what she is. I mean when she looks at me with that one eye seeing and one eye blind I don't know what she sees. I see you go about with her like she was any child, and I think, What are they? What's the strength of that woman, for she's not a fool, to hold a fire by the hand, to spin thread with the whirlwind? They say, mistress, that you lived as a child yourself with the Old Ones, the Dark Ones, the Ones Underfoot, and that you were queen and servant of those powers. Maybe that's why you're not afraid of this one. What power she is, I don't know, I don't say. But it's beyond my teaching, I know that—or Beech's, or any witch or wizard I ever knew! I'll give you my advice, mistress, free and feeless. It's this: Beware.

Beware her, the day she finds her strength! That's all."

"I thank you, Mistress Ivy," Tenar said with all the formality of the Priestess of the Tombs of Atuan, and went out of the warm room into the thin, biting wind of the end of autumn.

She was still angry. Nobody would help her, she thought. She knew the job was beyond her, they didn't have to tell her that—but none of them would help her. Ogion had died, and old Moss ranted, and Ivy warned, and Beech kept clear, and Ged—the one who might really have helped—Ged ran away. Ran off like a whipped dog, and never sent sign or word to her, never gave a thought to her or Therru, but only to his own precious shame. That was his child, his nurseling. That was all he cared about. He had never cared or thought about her, only about power—her power, his power, how he could use it, how he could make more power of it. Putting the broken Ring together, making the Rune, putting a king on the throne. And when his power was gone, still it was all he could think about: that it was gone, lost, leaving him only himself, his shame, his emptiness.

You aren't being fair, Goha said to Tenar.

Fair! said Tenar. Did he play fair?

Yes, said Goha. He did. Or tried to.

Well, then, he can play fair with the goats he's herding; it's nothing to me, said Tenar, trudging homeward in the wind and the first, sparse, cold rain.

"Snow tonight, maybe," said her tenant Tiff, meeting her on the road beside the meadows of the Kaheda.

"Snow so soon? I hope not."

"Freeze, anyway, for sure."

And it froze when the sun was down: rain puddles and watering troughs skimming over, then opaqued with ice; the reeds by the Kaheda stilled, bound in ice; the wind itself stilled as if frozen, unable to move.

Beside the fire—a sweeter fire than Ivy's, for the wood was that of an old apple that had been taken down in the orchard last spring—Tenar and Therru sat to spin and talk after supper was cleared away.

"Tell the story about the cat ghosts," Therru said in her husky voice as she started the wheel to spin a mass of dark, silky goat's-wool into fleecefell yarn.

"That's a summer story."

Therru cocked her head.

"In winter the stories should be the great stories. In winter you learn the *Creation of Éa,* so that you can sing it at the Long Dance when summer comes. In winter you learn the Winter Carol and the *Deed of the Young King,* and at the Festival of Sunreturn, when the sun turns north to bring the spring, you can sing them."

"I can't sing," the girl whispered.

Tenar was winding spun yarn off the distaff into a ball, her hands deft and rhythmic.

"Not only the voice sings," she said. "The mind

sings. The prettiest voice in the world's no good if the mind doesn't know the songs." She untied the last bit of yarn, which had been the first spun. "You have strength, Therru, and strength that is ignorant is dangerous."

"Like the ones who wouldn't learn," Therru said. "The wild ones." Tenar did not know what she meant, and looked her question. "The ones that stayed in the west," Therru said.

"Ah—the dragons—in the song of the Woman of Kemay. Yes. Exactly. So: which will we start with—how the islands were raised from the sea, or how King Morred drove back the Black Ships?"

"The islands," Therru whispered. Tenar had rather hoped she would choose the *Deed of the Young King*, for she saw Lebannen's face as Morred's; but the child's choice was the right one. "Very well," she said. She glanced up at Ogion's great Lore-books on the mantel, encouraging herself that if she forgot, she could find the words there; and drew breath; and began.

By her bedtime Therru knew how Segoy had raised the first of the islands from the depths of Time. Instead of singing to her, Tenar sat on the bed after tucking her in, and they recited together, softly, the first stanza of the song of the Making.

Tenar carried the little oil lamp back to the kitchen, listening to the absolute silence. The frost had bound the world, locked it. No star showed.

Blackness pressed at the single window of the kitchen. Cold lay on the stone floors.

She went back to the fire, for she was not sleepy yet. The great words of the song had stirred her spirit, and there was still anger and unrest in her from her talk with Ivy. She took the poker to rouse up a little flame from the backlog. As she struck the log, there was an echo of the sound in the back of the house.

She straightened up and stood listening.

Again: a soft, dull thump or thud—outside the house—at the dairy window?

The poker still in her hand, Tenar went down the dark hall to the door that gave on the cool-room. Beyond the cool-room was the dairy. The house was built against a low hill, and both those rooms ran back into the hill like cellars, though on a level with the rest of the house. The cool-room had only air-vents; the dairy had a door and a window, low and wide like the kitchen window, in its one outside wall. Standing at the cool-room door, she could hear that window being pried or jimmied, and men's voices whispering.

Flint had been a methodical householder. Every door but one of his house had a bar-bolt on each side of it, a stout length of cast iron set in slides. All were kept clean and oiled; none were ever locked.

She slipped the bolt across the cool-room door. It slid into place without a sound, fitting snug into the heavy iron slot on the doorjamb.

She heard the outer door of the dairy opened. One of them had finally thought to try it, before they broke the window, and found it wasn't locked. She heard the mutter of voices again. Then silence, long enough that she heard her heartbeat drumming in her ears so loud she feared she could not hear any sound over it. She felt her legs trembling and trembling, and felt the cold of the floor creep up under her skirt like a hand.

"It's open," a man's voice whispered near her, and her heart leapt painfully. She put her hand on the bolt, thinking it was open—she had unlocked not locked it— She had almost slid it back when she heard the door between the cool-room and the dairy creak, opening. She knew that creak of the upper hinge. She knew the voice that had spoken, too, but in a different way of knowing. "It's a storeroom," Handy said, and then, as the door she stood against rattled against the bolt, "This one's locked." It rattled again. A thin blade of light, like a knife blade, flicked between the door and the jamb. It touched her breast, and she drew back as if it had cut her.

The door rattled again, but not much. It was solid, solidly hinged, and the bolt was firm.

They muttered together on the other side of the door. She knew they were planning to come around and try the front of the house. She found herself at the front door, bolting it, not knowing how she came there. Maybe this was a nightmare. She had had this dream, that they were trying to get into the house, that they drove thin knives through the cracks of the doors. The doors—was there any other door they could get in? The windows—the shutters of the bedroom windows— Her breath came so short she thought she could not get to Therru's room, but she was there, she brought the heavy wooden shutters across the glass. The hinges were stiff, and they came together with a bang. Now they knew. Now they were coming. They would come to the window of the next room, her room. They would be there before she could close the shutters. And they were.

She saw the faces, blurs moving in the darkness outside, as she tried to free the left-hand shutter from its hasp. It was stuck. She could not make it move. A hand touched the glass, flattening white against it.

"There she is."

"Let us in. We won't hurt you."

"We just want to talk to you."

"He just wants to see his little girl."

She got the shutter free and dragged it across the window. But if they broke the glass they would be able to push the shutters open from the outside. The fastening was only a hook that would pull out of the wood if forced.

"Let us in and we won't hurt you," one of the voices said.

She heard their feet on the frozen ground, crackling in the fallen leaves. Was Therru awake? The crash of the shutters closing might have wakened her, but she had made no sound. Tenar stood in the doorway between her room and Therru's. It was pitch-dark, silent. She was afraid to touch the child and waken her. She must stay in the room with her. She must fight for her. She had had the poker in her hand, where had she put it? She had put it down to close the shutters. She could not find it. She groped for it in the blackness of the room that seemed to have no walls.

The front door, which led into the kitchen, rattled, shaken in its frame.

If she could find the poker she would stay in here, she would fight them.

"Here!" one of them called, and she knew what he had found. He was looking up at the kitchen window, broad, unshuttered, easy to reach.

She went, very slowly it seemed, groping, to the door of the room. It was Therru's room now. It had been her children's room. The nursery. That was why there was no lock on the inner side of the door. So the children could not lock themselves in and be frightened if the bolt stuck.

Around back of the hill, through the orchard, Clearbrook and Shandy would be asleep in their cottage. If she called, maybe Shandy would hear. If she opened the bedroom window and called—or if she waked Therru and they climbed out the window and ran through the orchard—but the men were there, right there, waiting.

It was more than she could bear. The frozen terror that had bound her broke, and in rage she ran into the kitchen that was all red light in her eyes, grabbed up the long, sharp butcher knife from the block, flung back the door-bolt, and stood in the doorway. "Come on, then!" she said.

As she spoke there was a howl and a sucking gasp, and a man yelled, "Look out!" Another shouted, "Here! Here!"

Then there was silence.

Light from the open doorway shot across the black ice of puddles, glittered on the black branches of the oaks and on fallen silver leaves, and as her eyes cleared she saw that something was crawling towards her on the path, a dark mass or heap crawling towards her, making a high, sobbing wail. Behind the light a black shape ran and darted, and long blades shone.

"Tenar!"

"Stop there," she said, raising the knife.

"Tenar! It's me—Hawk, Sparrowhawk!"

"Stay there," she said.

The darting black shape stood still next to the black mass lying on the path. The light from the doorway shone dim on a body, a face, a long-tined pitchfork held upright, like a wizard's staff, she thought. "Is that you?" she said.

He was kneeling now by the black thing on the path.

"I killed him, I think," he said. He looked over

his shoulder, stood up. There was no sign or sound of the other men.

"Where are they?"

"Ran. Give me a hand, Tenar."

She held the knife in one hand. With the other she took hold of the arm of the man that lay huddled up on the path. Ged took him under the shoulder and they dragged him up the step and into the house. He lay on the stone floor of the kitchen, and blood ran out of his chest and belly like water from a pitcher. His upper lip was drawn back from his teeth, and only the whites of his eyes showed.

"Lock the door," Ged said, and she locked the door.

"Linens in the press," she said, and he got a sheet and tore it for bandages, which she bound round and round the man's belly and breast, into which three of the four tines of the pitchfork had driven full force, making three ragged springs of blood that dripped and squirted as Ged supported the man's torso so that she could wrap the bandages.

"What are you doing here? Did you come with them?"

"Yes. But they didn't know it. That's about all you can do, Tenar." He let the man's body sag down, and sat back, breathing hard, wiping his face with the back of his bloody hand. "I think I killed him," he said again.

"Maybe you did." Tenar watched the bright red

spots spread slowly on the heavy linen that wrapped the man's thin, hairy chest and belly. She stood up, and swayed, very dizzy. "Get by the fire," she said. "You must be perishing."

She did not know how she had known him in the dark outside. By his voice, maybe. He wore a bulky shepherd's winter coat of cut fleece with the leather side out, and a shepherd's knit watch cap pulled down; his face was lined and weathered, his hair long and iron-grey. He smelled like woodsmoke, and frost, and sheep. He was shivering, his whole body shaking. "Get by the fire," she said again. "Put wood on it."

He did so. Tenar filled the kettle and swung it out on its iron arm over the blaze.

There was blood on her skirt, and she used an end of linen soaked in cold water to clean it. She gave the cloth to Ged to clean the blood off his hands. "What do you mean," she said, "you came with them but they didn't know it?"

"I was coming down. From the mountain. On the road from the springs of the Kaheda." He spoke in a flat voice as if out of breath, and his shivering made his speech slur. "Heard men behind me, and I went aside. Into the woods. Didn't feel like talking. I don't know. Something about them. I was afraid of them."

She nodded impatiently and sat down across the hearth from him, leaning forward to listen, her hands clenched tight in her lap. Her damp skirt was cold against her legs.

"I heard one of them say 'Oak Farm' as they went by. After that I followed them. One of them kept talking. About the child."

"What did he say?"

He was silent. He said finally, "That he was going to get her back. Punish her, he said. And get back at you. For stealing her, he said. He said—" He stopped.

"That he'd punish me, too."

"They all talked. About, about that."

"That one isn't Handy." She nodded toward the man on the floor. "Is it the . . ."

"He said she was his." Ged looked at the man too, and back at the fire. "He's dying. We should get help."

"He won't die," Tenar said. "I'll send for Ivy in the morning. The others are still out there—how many of them?"

"Two."

"If he dies he dies, if he lives he lives. Neither of us is going out." She got to her feet, in a spasm of fear. "Did you bring in the pitchfork, Ged!"

He pointed to it, the four long tines shining as it leaned against the wall beside the door.

She sat down in the hearthseat again, but now she was shaking, trembling from head to foot, as he had done. He reached across the hearth to touch her arm. "It's all right," he said.

"What if they're still out there?"

"They ran."

"They could come back."

"Two against two? And we've got the pitchfork."

She lowered her voice to a bare whisper to say, in terror, "The pruning hook and the scythes are in the barn lean-to."

He shook his head. "They ran. They saw—him—and you in the door."

"What did you do?"

"He came at me. So I came at him."

"I mean, before. On the road."

"They got cold, walking. It started to rain, and they got cold, and started talking about coming here. Before that it was only this one, talking about the child and you, about teaching—teaching lessons—" His voice dried up. "I'm thirsty," he said.

"So am I. The kettle's not boiling yet. Go on."

He took breath and tried to tell his story coherently. "The other two didn't listen to him much. Heard it all before, maybe. They were in a hurry to get on. To get to Valmouth. As if they were running from somebody. Getting away. But it got cold, and he went on about Oak Farm, and the one with the cap said, 'Well, why not just go there and spend the night with—'"

"With the widow, yes."

Ged put his face in his hands. She waited.

He looked into the fire, and went on steadily. "Then I lost them for a while. The road came out level into the valley, and I couldn't follow along the way I'd been doing, in the woods, just behind them. I had to go aside, through the fields, keeping out of their sight. I don't know the country here, only the road. I was afraid if I cut across the fields I'd get lost, miss the house. And it was getting dark. I thought I'd missed the house, overshot it. I came back to the road, and almost ran into them—at the turn there. They'd seen the old man go by. They decided to wait till it was dark and they were sure nobody else was coming. They waited in the barn. I stayed outside. Just through the wall from them."

"You must be frozen," Tenar said dully.

"It was cold." He held his hands to the fire as if the thought of it had chilled him again. "I found the pitchfork by the lean-to door. They went around to the back of the house when they came out. I could have come to the front door then to warn you, it's what I should have done, but all I could think of was to take them by surprise—I thought it was my only advantage, chance. . . . I thought the house would be locked and they'd have to break in. But then I heard them going in, at the back, there. I went in—into the dairy—after them. I only just got out, when they came to the locked door." He gave a kind of laugh. "They went right by me in the dark. I could have tripped them. . . . One of them had a flint and steel, he'd burn a little tinder when they wanted to see a lock. They came around front. I heard you putting up the shutters; I knew you'd heard them. They talked about smashing the window they'd seen you at. Then the one with the cap saw the window—that window—" He nodded toward the kitchen window, with its deep, broad inner sill. "He said, 'Get me a rock, I'll smash that right open,' and they came to where he was, and they were about to hoist him up to the sill. So I let out a yell, and he dropped down, and one of them—this one—came running right at me.

"Ah, ah," gasped the man lying on the floor, as if telling Ged's tale for him. Ged got up and bent over him.

"He's dying, I think."

"No, he's not," Tenar said. She could not stop shaking entirely, but it was only an inward tremor now. The kettle was singing. She made a pot of tea, and laid her hands on the thick pottery sides of the teapot while it steeped. She poured out two cups, then a third, into which she put a little cold water. "It's too hot to drink," she told Ged, "hold it a minute first. I'll see if this'll go into him." She sat down on the floor by the man's head, lifted it on one arm, put the cup of cooled tea to his mouth, pushed the rim between the bared teeth. The warm stuff ran into his mouth; he swallowed. "He won't die," she said. "The floor's like ice. Help me move him nearer the fire."

Ged started to take the rug from a bench that ran along the wall between the chimney and the hall. "Don't use that, it's a good piece of weaving," Tenar said, and she went to the closet and brought out a worn-out felt cloak, which she spread out as a bed for the man. They hauled the inert body onto it, lapped it over him. The soaked red spots on the bandages had grown no larger.

Tenar stood up, and stood motionless.

"Therru," she said.

Ged looked round, but the child was not there. Tenar went hurriedly out of the room.

The children's room, the child's room, was perfectly dark and quiet. She felt her way to the bed, and laid her hand on the warm curve of the blanket over Therru's shoulder.

"Therru?"

The child's breathing was peaceful. She had not waked. Tenar could feel the heat of her body, like a radiance in the cold room.

As she went out, Tenar ran her hand across the chest of drawers and touched cold metal: the poker she had laid down when she closed the shutters. She brought it back to the kitchen, stepped over the man's body, and hung the poker on its hook on the chimney. She stood looking down at the fire.

"I couldn't do anything," she said. "What should I have done? Run out—right away—shouted, and run to Clearbrook and Shandy. They wouldn't have had time to hurt Therru."

"They would have been in the house with her, and you outside it, with the old man and woman. Or they could have picked her up and gone clear away with her. You did what you could. What you did was right. Timed right. The light from the house, and you coming out with the knife, and me there—they could see the pitchfork then—and him down. So they ran."

"Those that could," said Tenar. She turned and stirred the man's leg a little with the toe of her shoe, as if he were an object she was a little curious about, a little repelled by, like a dead viper. "*You* did the right thing," she said.

"I don't think he even saw it. He ran right onto it. It was like—" He did not say what it was like. He said, "Drink your tea," and poured himself more from the pot keeping warm on the hearthbricks. "It's good. Sit down," he said, and she did so.

"When I was a boy," he said after a time, "the Kargs raided my village. They had lances—long, with feathers tied to the shaft—"

She nodded. "Warriors of the God-Brothers," she said.

"I made a . . . a fog-spell. To confuse them. But they came on, some of them. I saw one of them run right onto a pitchfork—like him. Only it went clear through him. Below the waist."

"You hit a rib," Tenar said.

He nodded.

"It was the only mistake you made," she said. Her teeth were chattering now. She drank her tea. "Ged," she said, "what if they come back?"

"They won't."

"They could set fire to the house."

"This house?" He looked around at the stone walls.

"The haybarn—"

"They won't be back," he said, doggedly.

"No."

They held their cups with care, warming their hands on them.

"She slept through it."

"It's well she did."

"But she'll see him—here—in the morning—"

They stared at each other.

"If I'd killed him—if he'd die!" Ged said with rage. "I could drag him out and bury him—"

"Do it."

He merely shook his head angrily.

"What does it matter, why, why can't we do it!" Tenar demanded.

"I don't know."

"As soon as it gets light—"

"I'll get him out of the house. Wheelbarrow. The old man can help me."

"He can't lift anything any more. I'll help you."

"However I can do it, I'll cart him off to the village. There's a healer of some kind there?"

"A witch, Ivy."

She felt all at once abysmally, infinitely weary. She could scarcely hold the cup in her hand.

"There's more tea," she said, thick-tongued.

He poured himself another cupful.

The fire danced in her eyes. The flames swam, flared up, sank away, brightened again against the sooty stone, against the dark sky, against the pale sky, the gulfs of evening, the depths of air and light beyond the world. Flames of yellow, orange, orange-red, red tongues of flame, flame-tongues, the words she could not speak.

"Tenar."

"We call the star Tehanu," she said.

"Tenar, my dear. Come on. Come with me."

They were not at the fire. They were in the dark—in the dark hall. The dark passage. They had been there before, leading each other, following each other, in the darkness underneath the earth.

"This is the way," she said.

WINTER

SHE WAS WAKING, NOT WANTING to waken. Faint grey shone at the window in thin slits through the shutters. Why was the window shuttered? She got up hurriedly and went down the hall to the kitchen. No one sat by the fire, no one lay on the floor. There was no sign of anyone, anything. Except the teapot and three cups on the counter.

Therru got up about sunrise, and they breakfasted as usual; clearing up, the girl asked, "What happened?" She lifted a corner of wet linen from the soaking-tub in the pantry. The water in the tub was veined and clouded with brownish red.

"Oh, my period came on early," Tenar said, startled at the lie as she spoke it.

Therru stood a moment motionless, her nostrils flared and her head still, like an animal getting a scent. Then she dropped the sheeting back into the water, and went out to feed the chickens.

Tenar felt ill; her bones ached. The weather was still cold, and she stayed indoors as much as she could. She tried to keep Therru in, but when the sun came out with a keen, bright wind, Therru wanted to be out in it.

"Stay with Shandy in the orchard," Tenar said.

Therru said nothing as she slipped out.

The burned and deformed side of her face was made rigid by the destruction of muscles and the thickness of the scar-surface, but as the scars got older and as Tenar learned by long usage not to look away from it as deformity but to see it as face, it had expressions of its own. When Therru was frightened, the burned and darkened side "closed in," as Tenar thought, drawing together, hardening. When she was excited or intent, even the blind eye socket seemed to gaze, and the scars reddened and were hot to touch. Now, as she went out, there was a queer look to her, as if her face were not human at all, an animal, some strange horny-skinned wild creature with one bright eye, silent, escaping.

And Tenar knew that as she had lied to her for the first time, Therru for the first time was going to disobey her. The first but not the last time.

She sat down at the fireside with a weary sigh, and did nothing at all for a while.

A rap at the door: Clearbrook and Ged—no, Hawk she must call him—Hawk standing on the doorstep. Old Clearbrook was full of talk and importance, Ged dark and quiet and bulky in his grimy sheepskin coat. "Come in," she said. "Have some tea. What's the news?"

"Tried to get away, down to Valmouth, but the men from Kahedanan, the bailies, come down and 'twas in Cherry's outhouse they found 'em," Clearbrook announced, waving his fist.

"He escaped?" Horror caught at her.

"The other two," Ged said. "Not him."

"See, they found the body up in the old shambles on Round Hill, all beat to pieces like, up in the old shambles there, by Kahedanan, so ten, twelve of 'em 'pointed theirselves bailies then and there and come after them. And there was a search all through the villages last night, and this morning before 'twas hardly light they found 'em hiding out in Cherry's outhouse. Half-froze they was."

"He's dead, then?" she asked, bewildered.

Ged had shucked off the heavy coat and was now sitting on the cane-bottom chair by the door to undo his leather gaiters. "*He's* alive," he said in his quiet voice. "Ivy has him. I took him in this morning on the muck-cart. There were people out on the road before daylight, hunting for all three of them. They'd killed a woman, up in the hills."

"What woman?" Tenar whispered.

Her eyes were on Ged's. He nodded slightly.

Clearbrook wanted the story to be his, and took it up loudly: "I talked with some o' them from up there and they told me they'd all four of 'em been traipsing and camping and vagranting about near Kahedanan, and the woman would come into the village to beg, all beat about and burns and bruises all over her. They'd send her in, the men would, see, like that to beg, and then she'd go back to 'em, and she told people if she went back with nothing they'd beat her more, so they said why go back? But if she didn't they'd come after her, she said, see, and she'd always go with 'em. But then they finally went too far and beat her to death, and they took and left her body in the old shambles there where there's still some o' the stink left, you know, maybe thinking that was hiding what they done. And they came away then, down here, just last night. And why didn't you shout and call last night, Goha? Hawk says they was right here, sneaking about the house, when he come on 'em. I surely would have heard, or Shandy would, her ears might be sharper than mine. Did you tell her yet?"

Tenar shook her head.

"I'll just go tell her," said the old man, delighted to be first with the news, and he clumped off across the yard. He turned back halfway. "Never would have picked you as useful with a pitchfork!" he shouted to Ged, and slapped his thigh, laughing, and went on.

Ged slipped off the heavy gaiters, took off his muddy shoes and set them on the doorstep, and came over to the fire in his stocking feet. Trousers and jerkin and shirt of homespun wool: a Gontish goatherd, with a canny face, a hawk nose, and clear, dark eyes.

"There'll be people out soon," he said. "To tell you all about it, and hear what happened here again. They've got the two that ran off shut up now in a wine cellar with no wine in it, and fifteen or twenty men guarding them, and twenty or thirty boys trying to get a peek. . . ." He yawned, shook his shoulders and arms to loosen them, and with a glance at Tenar asked permission to sit down at the fire.

She gestured to the hearthseat. "You must be worn out," she whispered.

"I slept a little, here, last night. Couldn't stay awake." He yawned again. He looked up at her, gauging, seeing how she was.

"It was Therru's mother," she said. Her voice would not go above a whisper.

He nodded. He sat leaning forward a bit, his arms on his knees, as Flint had used to sit, gazing into the fire. They were very alike and entirely unlike, as unlike as a buried stone and a soaring bird. Her heart ached, and her bones ached, and her mind was bewildered among foreboding and grief and remembered fear and a troubled lightness.

"The witch has got our man," he said. "Tied down in case he feels lively. With the holes in him stuffed full of spiderwebs and blood-stanching spells. She says he'll live to hang."

"To hang."

"It's up to the King's Courts of Law, now that they're meeting again. Hanged or set to slave-labor."

She shook her head, frowning.

"You wouldn't just let him go, Tenar," he said gently, watching her.

"No."

"They must be punished," he said, still watching her.

" 'Punished.' That's what *he* said. Punish the child. She's bad. She must be punished. Punish me, for taking her. For being—" She struggled to speak. "I don't want punishment! — It should not have happened. — I wish you'd killed him!"

"I did my best," Ged said.

After a good while she laughed, rather shakily. "You certainly did."

"Think how easy it would have been," he said, looking into the coals again, "when I was a wizard. I could have set a binding spell on them, up there on the road, before they knew it. I could have marched them right down to Valmouth like a flock of sheep. Or last night, here, think of the fireworks I could have set off! They'd never have known what hit them."

"They still don't," she said.

He glanced at her. There was in his eye the faintest, irrepressible gleam of triumph.

"No," he said. "They don't."

"Useful with a pitchfork," she murmured.

He yawned enormously.

"Why don't you go in and get some sleep? The second room down the hall. Unless you want to entertain company. I see Lark and Daisy coming, and some of the children." She had got up, hearing voices, to look out the window.

"I'll do that," he said, and slipped away.

Lark and her husband, Daisy the blacksmith's wife, and other friends from the village came by all day long to tell and be told all, as Ged had said. She found that their company revived her, carried her away from the constant presence of last night's terror, little by little, till she could begin to look back on it as something that had happened, not something that was happening, that must always be happening to her.

That was also what Therru had to learn to do, she thought, but not with one night: with her life.

She said to Lark when the others had gone, "What makes me rage at myself is how stupid I was."

"I did tell you you ought to keep the house locked."

"No—Maybe—That's just it."

"I know," said Lark.

"But I meant, when they were here—I could have run out and fetched Shandy and Clearbrook—maybe I could have taken Therru. Or I could have gone to the lean-to and got the pitchfork myself. Or the apple-pruner. It's seven feet long with a blade like a razor; I keep it the way Flint kept it. Why didn't I do that? Why didn't I do something? Why did I just lock myself in—when it wasn't any good trying to? If he— If Hawk hadn't been here— All I did was trap myself and Therru. I did finally go to the door with the butcher knife, and I shouted at them. I was half crazy. But that wouldn't have scared them off."

"I don't know," Lark said. "It was crazy, but maybe . . . I don't know. What could you do but lock the doors? But it's like we're all our lives locking the doors. It's the house we live in."

They looked around at the stone walls, the stone floors, the stone chimney, the sunny window of the kitchen of Oak Farm, Farmer Flint's house.

"That girl, that woman they murdered," Lark said, looking shrewdly at Tenar. "She was the same one."

Tenar nodded.

"One of them told me she was pregnant. Four, five months along."

They were both silent.

"Trapped," Tenar said.

Lark sat back, her hands on the skirt on her heavy thighs, her back straight, her handsome face set. "Fear," she said. "What are we so afraid of? Why do we let 'em tell us we're afraid? What is it *they're* afraid of?" She picked up the stocking she had been darning, turned it in her hands, was silent awhile; finally she said, "What are they afraid of us for?"

Tenar spun and did not answer.

Therru came running in, and Lark greeted her: "There's my honey! Come give me a hug, my honey girl!"

Therru hugged her hastily. "Who are the men they caught?" she demanded in her hoarse, toneless voice, looking from Lark to Tenar.

Tenar stopped her wheel. She spoke slowly.

"One was Handy. One was a man called Shag. The one that was hurt is called Hake." She kept her eyes on Therru's face; she saw the fire, the scar reddening. "The woman they killed was called Senny, I think."

"Senini," the child whispered.

Tenar nodded.

"Did they kill her dead?"

She nodded again.

"Tadpole says they were *here*."

She nodded again.

The child looked around the room, as the women had done; but her look was utterly unacceptant, seeing no walls.

"Will you kill them?"

"They may be hanged."

"Dead?"

"Yes."

Therru nodded, half indifferently. She went out again, rejoining Lark's children by the well-house.

The two women said nothing. They spun and mended, silent, by the fire, in Flint's house.

After a long time Lark said, "What's become of the fellow, the shepherd, that followed 'em here? Hawk, you said he's called?"

"He's asleep in there," said Tenar, nodding to the back of the house.

"Ah," said Lark.

The wheel purred. "I knew him before last night."

"Ah. Up at Re Albi, did you?"

Tenar nodded. The wheel purred.

"To follow those three, and take 'em on in the dark with a pitchfork, that took a bit of courage, now. Not a young man, is he?"

"No." After a while she went on, "He'd been ill, and needed work. So I sent him over the mountain to tell Clearbrook to take him on here. But Clearbrook thinks he can still do it all himself, so he sent him up above the Springs for the summer herding. He was coming back from that."

"Think you'll keep him on here, then?"

"If he likes," said Tenar.

Another group came out to Oak Farm from the village, wanting to hear Goha's story and tell her their part in the great capture of the murderers, and look at the pitchfork and compare its four long tines to the three bloody spots on the bandages of the man called Hake, and talk it all over again. Tenar was glad to see the evening come, and call Therru in, and shut the door.

She raised her hand to latch it. She lowered her hand and forced herself to turn from it, leaving it unlocked.

"Sparrowhawk's in your room," Therru informed her, coming back to the kitchen with eggs from the cool-room.

"I meant to tell you he was here—I'm sorry."

"I know him," Therru said, washing her face and hands in the pantry. And when Ged came in, heavy-eyed and unkempt, she went straight to him and put up her arms.

"Therru," he said, and took her up and held her. She clung to him briefly, then broke free.

"I know the beginning part of the *Creation*," she told him.

"Will you sing it to me?" Again glancing at Tenar for permission, he sat down in his place at the hearth.

"I can only say it."

He nodded and waited, his face rather stern. The child said:

The making from the unmaking,
The ending from the beginning,
Who shall know surely?
What we know is the doorway between them
that we enter departing.
Among all beings ever returning,
the eldest, the Doorkeeper, Segoy. . . .

The child's voice was like a metal brush drawn across metal, like dry leaves, like the hiss of fire burning. She spoke to the end of the first stanza:

Then from the foam bright Éa broke.

Ged nodded brief, firm approval. "Good," he said.

"Last night," Tenar said. "Last night she learned it. It seems a year ago."

"I can learn more," said Therru.

"You will," Ged told her.

"Now finish cleaning the squash, please," said Tenar, and the child obeyed.

"What shall I do?" Ged asked. Tenar paused, looking at him.

"I need that kettle filled and heated."

He nodded, and took the kettle to the pump.

They made and ate their supper and cleared it away.

"Say the *Making* again as far as you know it," Ged said to Therru, at the hearth, "and we'll go on from there."

She said the second stanza once with him, once with Tenar, once by herself.

"Bed," said Tenar.

"You didn't tell Sparrowhawk about the king."

"You tell him," Tenar said, amused at this pretext for delay.

Therru turned to Ged. Her face, scarred and

whole, seeing and blind, was intent, fiery. "The king came in a ship. He had a sword. He gave me the bone dolphin. His ship was flying, but I was sick, because Handy touched me. But the king touched me there and the mark went away." She showed her round, thin arm. Tenar stared. She had forgotten the mark.

"Some day I want to fly to where he lives," Therru told Ged. He nodded. "I will do that," she said. "Do you know him?"

"Yes. I know him. I went on a long journey with him."

"Where?"

"To where the sun doesn't rise and the stars don't set. And back from that place."

"Did you fly?"

He shook his head. "I can only walk," he said.

The child pondered, and then as if satisfied said, "Good night," and went off to her room. Tenar followed her; but Therru did not want to be sung to sleep. "I can say the *Making* in the dark," she said. "*Both* stanzas."

Tenar came back to the kitchen and sat down again across the hearth from Ged.

"How she's changing!" she said. "I can't keep up with her. I'm old to be bringing up a child. And she . . . She obeys me, but only because she wants to."

"It's the only justification for obedience," Ged observed.

"But when she does take it into her head to

disobey me, what can I do? There's a wildness in her. Sometimes she's my Therru, sometimes she's something else, out of reach. I asked Ivy if she'd think of training her. Beech suggested it. Ivy said no. 'Why not?' I said. 'I'm afraid of her!' she said. . . . But you're not afraid of her. Nor she of you. You and Lebannen are the only men she's let touch her. *I* let that—that Handy—I can't talk about it. Oh, I'm tired! I don't understand anything. . . ."

Ged laid a knot on the fire to burn small and slow, and they both watched the leap and flutter of the flames.

"I'd like you to stay here, Ged," she said. "If you like."

He did not answer at once. She said, "Maybe you're going on to Havnor—"

"No, no. I have nowhere to go. I was looking for work."

"Well, there's plenty to be done here. Clearbrook won't admit it, but his arthritis has about finished him for anything but gardening. I've been wanting help ever since I came back. I could have told the old blockhead what I thought of him for sending you off up the mountain that way, but it's no use. He wouldn't listen."

"It was a good thing for me," Ged said. "It was the time I needed."

"You were herding sheep?"

"Goats. Right up at the top of the grazings. A boy they had took sick, and Serry took me on, sent me up there the first day. They keep 'em up there high and late, so the underwool grows thick. This last month I had the mountain pretty much to myself. Serry sent me up that coat and some supplies, and said to keep the herd up as high as I could as long as I could. So I did. It was fine, up there."

"Lonely," she said.

He nodded, half smiling.

"You always have been alone."

"Yes, I have."

She said nothing. He looked at her.

"I'd like to work here," he said.

"That's settled, then," she said. After a while she added, "For the winter, anyway."

The frost was harder tonight. Their world was perfectly silent except for the whisper of the fire. The silence was like a presence between them. She lifted her head and looked at him.

"Well," she said, "which bed shall I sleep in, Ged? The child's, or yours?"

He drew breath. He spoke low. "Mine, if you will."

"I will."

The silence held him. She could see the effort he made to break from it. "If you'll be patient with me," he said.

"I have been patient with you for twenty-five years," she said. She looked at him and began to laugh. "Come—come on, my dear—Better late than never! I'm only an old woman. . . . Nothing is wasted, nothing is ever wasted. You taught me that." She stood up, and he stood; she put out her hands, and he took them. They embraced, and their embrace became close. They held each other so fiercely, so dearly, that they stopped knowing anything but each other. It did not matter which bed they meant to sleep in. They lay that night on the hearthstones, and there she taught Ged the mystery that the wisest man could not teach him.

He built up the fire once, and fetched the good weaving off the bench. Tenar made no objection this time. Her cloak and his sheepskin coat were their blankets.

They woke again at dawn. A faint silvery light lay on the dark, half-leafless branches of the oaks outside the window. Tenar stretched out full length to feel his warmth against her. After a while she murmured, "He was lying here. Hake. Right under us. . . ."

Ged made a small noise of protest.

"Now you're a man indeed," she said. "Stuck another man full of holes, first, and lain with a woman, second. That's the proper order, I suppose."

"Hush," he murmured, turning to her, laying his head on her shoulder. "Don't."

"I will, Ged. Poor man! There's no mercy in me, only justice. I wasn't trained to mercy. Love is the only grace I have. Oh, Ged, don't fear me! You were a man when I first saw you! It's not a weapon or a woman can make a man, or magery either, or any power, anything but himself."

They lay in warmth and sweet silence.

"Tell me something."

He murmured assent sleepily.

"How did you happen to hear what they were saying? Hake and Handy and the other one. How did you happen to be just there, just then?"

He raised himself up on one elbow so he could look at her face. His own face was so open and vulnerable in its ease and fulfillment and tenderness that she had to reach up and touch his mouth, there where she had kissed it first, months ago, which led to his taking her into his arms again, and the conversation was not continued in words.

There were formalities to be got through. The chief of them was to tell Clearbrook and the other tenants of Oak Farm that she had replaced "the old master" with a hired hand. She did so promptly and bluntly. They could not do anything about it, nor did it entail any threat to them. A widow's tenure of her husband's property was contingent on there being no male heir or claimant. Flint's son the seaman was the heir, and Flint's widow was merely holding the farm for him. If she died, it would go to Clearbrook to hold for the heir; if Spark never claimed it, it would go to a distant cousin of Flint's in Kahedanan. The two couples who did not own the land but held a life interest in the work and profit of the farming, as was common on Gont, could not be dislodged by any man the widow took up with, even if she married him; but she feared they might resent her lack of fidelity to Flint, whom they had after all known longer than she had. To her relief they made no objections at all. "Hawk" had won their approval with one jab of a pitchfork. Besides, it was only good sense in a woman to want a man in the house to protect her. If she took him into her bed, well, the appetites of widows were proverbial. And, after all, she was a foreigner.

The attitude of the villagers was much the same. A bit of whispering and sniggering, but little more. It seemed that being respectable was easier than Moss thought; or perhaps it was that used goods had little value.

She felt as soiled and diminished by their acceptance as she would have by their disapproval. Only Lark freed her from shame, by making no judgments at all, and using no words—man, woman, widow, foreigner—in place of what she saw, but simply looking, watching her and Hawk with interest, curiosity, envy, and generosity.

Because Lark did not see Hawk through the words herdsman, hired hand, widow's man, but looked at him himself, she saw a good deal that puzzled her. His dignity and simplicity were not greater than that of other men she had known, but were a little different in quality; there was a size to him, she thought, not height or girth, certainly, but soul and mind. She said to Ivy, "That man hasn't lived among goats all his life. He knows more about the world than he does about a farm."

"I'd say he's a sorcerer who's been accursed or lost his power some way," the witch said. "It happens."

"Ah," said Lark.

But the word "archmage" was too great and grand a word to bring from far-off pomps and palaces and fit to the dark-eyed, grey-haired man at Oak Farm, and she never did that. If she had, she could not have been as comfortable with him as she was. Even the idea of his having been a sorcerer made her a bit uneasy, the word getting in the way of the man, until she actually saw him again. He was up in one of the old apple trees in the orchard pruning out deadwood, and he called out a greeting to her as she came to the farm. His name fit him well, she thought, perched up there, and she waved at him, and smiled as she went on.

Tenar had not forgotten the question she had asked him on the hearthstones under the sheepskin coat. She asked it again, a few days or months later—time went along very sweet and easy for them in the stone house, on the winterbound farm. "You never told me," she said, "how you came to hear them talking on the road."

"I told you, I think. I'd gone aside, hidden, when I heard men coming behind me."

"Why?"

"I was alone, and knew there were some gangs around."

"Yes, of course— But then just as they passed, Hake was talking about Therru?"

"He said 'Oak Farm,' I think."

"It's all perfectly possible. It just seems so convenient."

Knowing she did not disbelieve him, he lay back and waited.

"It's the kind of thing that happens to a wizard," she said.

"And others."

"Maybe."

"My dear, you're not trying to . . . reinstate me?"

"No. No, not at all. Would that be a sensible thing to do? If you were a wizard, would you be here?"

They were in the big oak-framed bed, well covered with sheepskins and feather-coverlets, for the room had no fireplace and the night was one of hard frost on fallen snow.

"But what I want to know is this. Is there something besides what you call power—that comes before it, maybe? Or something that power is just one way of using? Like this. Ogion said of you once that before you'd had any learning or training as a wizard at all, you were a mage. Mage-born, he said. So I imagined that, to have power, one must first have room for the power. An emptiness to fill. And the greater the emptiness the more power can fill it. But if the power never was got, or was taken away, or was given away—still that would be there."

"That emptiness," he said.

"Emptiness is one word for it. Maybe not the right word."

"Potentiality?" he said, and shook his head. "What is able to be . . . to become."

"I think you were there on that road, just there just then, because of that—because that is what happens to you. You didn't make it happen. You didn't cause it. It wasn't because of your 'power.' It happened to you. Because of your—emptiness."

After a while he said, "This isn't far from what I was taught as a boy on Roke: that true magery lies in doing only what you must do. But this would go further. Not to do, but to be done to. . . ."

"I don't think that's quite it. It's more like what true doing rises from. Didn't you come and save my life—didn't you run a fork into Hake? That was 'doing,' all right, doing what you must do. . . ."

He pondered again, and finally asked her, "Is this a wisdom taught you when you were Priestess of the Tombs?"

"No." She stretched a little, gazing into the darkness. "Arha was taught that to be powerful she must sacrifice. Sacrifice herself and others. A bargain: give, and so get. And I cannot say that that's untrue. But my soul can't live in that narrow place—this for that, tooth for tooth, death for life. . . . There is a freedom beyond that. Beyond payment, retribution, redemption—beyond all the bargains and the balances, there is freedom."

"*The doorway between them,*" he said softly.

That night Tenar dreamed. She dreamed that she saw the doorway of the *Creation of Éa*. It was a little window of gnarled, clouded, heavy glass, set low in the west wall of an old house above the sea. The window was locked. It had been bolted shut. She wanted to open it, but there was a word or a key, something she had forgotten, a word, a key, a name, without which she could not open it. She sought for it in rooms of stone that grew smaller and darker till she found that Ged was holding her, trying to wake her and comfort her, saying, "It's all right, dear love, it will be all right!"

"I can't get free!" she cried, clinging to him.

He soothed her, stroking her hair; they lay back together, and he whispered, "Look."

The old moon had risen. Its white brilliance on the fallen snow was reflected into the room, for cold as it was Tenar would not have the shutters closed. All the air above them was luminous. They lay in shadow, but it seemed as if the ceiling were a mere veil between them and endless, silver, tranquil depths of light.

It was a winter of heavy snows on Gont, and a long winter. The harvest had been a good one. There was food for the animals and people, and not much to do but eat it and stay warm.

Therru knew the *Creation of Éa* all through. She

spoke the Winter Carol and the *Deed of the Young King* on the day of Sunreturn. She knew how to handle a piecrust, how to spin on the wheel, and how to make soap. She knew the name and use of every plant that showed above the snow, and a good deal of other lore, herbal and verbal, that Ged had stowed away in his head from his short apprenticeship with Ogion and his long years at the School on Roke. But he had not taken down the Runes or the Lore-books from the mantelpiece, nor had he taught the child any word of the Language of the Making.

He and Tenar spoke of this. She told him how she had taught Therru the one word, *tolk*, and then had stopped, for it had not seemed right, though she did not know why.

"I thought perhaps it was because I'd never truly spoken that language, never used it in magery. I thought perhaps she should learn it from a true speaker of it."

"No man is that."

"No woman is half that."

"I meant that only the dragons speak it as their native tongue."

"Do they learn it?"

Struck by the question, he was slow to answer, evidently calling to mind all he had been told and knew of the dragons. "I don't know," he said at last. "What do we know about them? Would they teach as we do, mother to child, elder to younger? Or are they like the animals, teaching some things, but born knowing most of what they know? Even that we don't know. But my guess would be that the dragon and the speech of the dragon are one. One being."

"And they speak no other tongue."

He nodded. "They do not learn," he said. "They are."

Therru came through the kitchen. One of her tasks was to keep the kindling box filled, and she was busy at it, bundled up in a cut-down lambskin jacket and cap, trotting back and forth from the woodhouse to the kitchen. She dumped her load in the box by the chimney corner and set off again.

"What is it she sings?" Ged asked.

"Therru?"

"When she's alone."

"But she never sings. She can't."

"Her way of singing. 'Farther west than west . . .' "

"Ah!" said Tenar. "That story! Did Ogion never tell you about the Woman of Kemay?"

"No," he said, "tell me."

She told him the tale as she spun, and the purr and hush of the wheel went along with the words of the story. At the end of it she said, "When the Master Windkey told me how he'd come looking for 'a woman on Gont,' I thought of her. But she'd be dead by now, no doubt. And how would a fisherwoman who was a dragon be an archmage, anyhow!"

"Well, the Patterner didn't say that a woman on Gont was to be archmage," said Ged. He was mending a badly torn pair of breeches, sitting up in the window ledge to get what light the dark day afforded. It was a half-month after Sunreturn and the coldest time yet.

"What did he say, then?"

"'A woman on Gont.' So you told me."

"But they were asking who was to be the next archmage."

"And got no answer to that question."

"*Infinite are the arguments of mages,*" said Tenar rather drily.

Ged bit the thread off and rolled the unused length around two fingers.

"I learned to quibble a bit, on Roke," he admitted. "But this isn't a quibble, I think. 'A woman on Gont' can't become archmage. No woman can be archmage. She'd unmake what she became in becoming it. The Mages of Roke are men—their power is the power of men, their knowledge is the knowledge of men. Both manhood and magery are built on one rock: power belongs to men. If women had power, what would men be but women who can't bear children? And what would women be but men who can?"

"Hah!" went Tenar; and presently, with some cunning, she said, "Haven't there been queens? Weren't they women of power?"

"A queen's only a she-king," said Ged.

She snorted.

"I mean, men give her power. They let her use their power. But it isn't hers, is it? It isn't because she's a woman that she's powerful, but despite it."

She nodded. She stretched, sitting back from the spinning wheel. "What is a woman's power, then?" she asked.

"I don't think we know."

"When has a woman power because she's a woman? With her children, I suppose. For a while . . ."

"In her house, maybe."

She looked around the kitchen. "But the doors are shut," she said, "the doors are locked."

"Because you're valuable."

"Oh, yes. We're precious. So long as we're powerless. . . . I remember when I first learned that! Kossil threatened me—me, the One Priestess of the Tombs. And I realized that I was helpless. I had the honor; but she had the power, from the God-king, the man. Oh, it made me angry! And frightened me. . . . Lark and I talked about this once. She said, 'Why are men *afraid* of women?'"

"If your strength is only the other's weakness, you live in fear," Ged said.

"Yes; but women seem to fear their own strength, to be afraid of themselves."

"Are they ever taught to trust themselves?" Ged asked, and as he spoke Therru came in on her work again. His eyes and Tenar's met.

"No," she said. "Trust is not what we're taught." She watched the child stack the wood in the box. "If power were trust," she said. "I like that word. If it weren't all these arrangements—one above the other—kings and masters and mages and owners—It all seems so unnecessary. Real power, real freedom, would lie in trust, not force."

"As children trust their parents," he said.

They were both silent.

"As things are," he said, "even trust corrupts. The men on Roke trust themselves and one another. Their power is pure, nothing taints its purity, and so they take that purity for wisdom. They cannot imagine doing wrong."

She looked up at him. He had never spoken about Roke thus before, from wholly outside it, free of it.

"Maybe they need some women there to point that possibility out to them," she said, and he laughed.

She restarted the wheel. "I still don't see why, if there can be she-kings, there can't be she-archmages."

Therru was listening.

"*Hot snow, dry water,*" said Ged, a Gontish saying. "Kings are given power by other men. A mage's power is his own—himself."

"And it's a male power. Because we don't even know what a woman's power is. All right. I see. But all the same, why can't they find an archmage—a he-archmage?"

Ged studied the tattered inseam of the breeches. "Well," he said, "if the Patterner wasn't answering their question, he was answering one they didn't ask. Maybe what they have to do is ask it."

"Is it a riddle?" Therru asked.

"Yes," said Tenar. "But we don't know the riddle. We only know the answer to it. The answer is: A woman on Gont."

"There's lots of them," Therru said after pondering a bit. Apparently satisfied by this, she went out for the next load of kindling.

Ged watched her go. "'All changed,'" he said. "'All . . . Sometimes I think, Tenar—I wonder if Lebannen's kingship is only a beginning. A doorway . . . And he the doorkeeper. Not to pass through."

"He seems so young," Tenar said, tenderly.

"Young as Morred was when he met the Black Ships. Young as I was when I . . ." He stopped, looking out the window at the grey, frozen fields through the leafless trees. "Or you, Tenar, in that dark place . . . What's youth or age? I don't know. Sometimes I feel as if I'd been alive for a thousand years; sometimes I feel my life's been like a flying swallow seen through the chink of a wall. I have died and been reborn, both in the dry land and here under the sun, more than once. And the *Making* tells us that we have all returned and return forever to the source, and that the source is ceaseless. *Only in dying, life.* . . . I thought about that when I was up with the goats on the mountain, and a day went on forever and yet no time passed before the evening came, and morning again. . . . I learned goat wisdom. So I thought, What is this grief of mine for? What man am I mourning? Ged the archmage? Why is Hawk the goatherd sick with grief and shame for him? What have I done that I should be ashamed?"

"Nothing," Tenar said. "Nothing, ever!"

"Oh, yes," said Ged. "All the greatness of men is founded on shame, made out of it. So Hawk the goatherd wept for Ged the archmage. And looked after the goats, also, as well as a boy his age could be expected to do. . . ."

After a while Tenar smiled. She said, a little shyly, "Moss said you were about fifteen."

"That would be about right. Ogion named me in the autumn; and the next summer I was off to Roke. . . . Who was that boy? An emptiness . . . A freedom."

"Who is Therru, Ged?"

He did not answer until she thought he was not going to answer, and then he said, "So made—what freedom is there for her?"

"We are our freedom, then?"

"I think so."

"You seemed, in your power, as free as man can be. But at what cost? What made you free? And I . . . I was made, molded like clay, by the will of the women serving the Old Powers, or serving the men who made all services and ways and places, I no longer know which. Then I went free, with you, for a moment, and with Ogion. But it was not *my* freedom. Only it gave me choice; and I chose. I chose to mold myself like clay to the use of a farm and a farmer and our children. I made myself a vessel. I know its shape. But not the clay. Life danced me. I know the dances. But I don't know who the dancer is."

"And she," Ged said after a long silence, "if she should ever dance—"

"They will fear her," Tenar whispered. Then the child came back in, and the conversation turned to the bread dough raising in the box by the stove. They talked so, quietly and long, passing from one thing to another and round and back, for half the brief day, often, spinning and sewing their lives together with words, the years and the deeds and the thoughts they had not shared. Then again they would be silent, working and thinking and dreaming, and the silent child was with them.

So the winter passed, till lambing season was on them, and the work got very heavy for a while as the days lengthened and grew bright. Then the swallows came from the isles under the sun, from the South Reach, where the star Gobardon shines in the constellation of Ending; but all the swallows' talk with one another was about beginning.

THE MASTER

LIKE THE SWALLOWS, THE SHIPS began to fly among the islands with the return of spring. In the villages there was talk, secondhand from Valmouth, of the king's ships harrying the harriers, driving well-established pirates to ruin, confiscating their ships and fortunes. Lord Heno himself sent out his three finest, fastest ships, captained by the sorcerer-seawolf Tally, who was feared by every merchantman from Soléa to the Andrades; his fleet was to ambush the king's ships off Oranéa and destroy them. But it was one of the king's ships that came into Valmouth Bay with Tally in chains aboard, and under orders to escort Lord Heno to Gont Port to be tried for piracy and murder. Heno barricaded himself in his stone manor house in the hills behind Valmouth, but neglected to light a fire, it being warm spring weather; so five or six of the king's young soldiers dropped in on him by way of the chimney, and the whole troop walked him chained through the streets of Valmouth and carried him off to justice.

When he heard this, Ged said with love and pride, "All that a king can do, he will do well."

Handy and Shag had been taken promptly off on the north road to Gont Port, and when his wounds healed enough Hake was carried there by ship, to be tried for murder at the king's courts of law. The news of their sentence to the galleys caused much satisfaction and self-congratulation in Middle Valley, to which Tenar, and Therru beside her, listened in silence.

There came other ships bearing other men sent by the king, not all of them popular among the townsfolk and villagers of rude Gont: royal sheriffs, sent to report on the system of bailiffs and officers of the peace and to hear complaints and grievances from the common people; tax reporters and tax collectors; noble visitors to the little lords of Gont, inquiring politely as to their fealty to the Crown in Havnor; and wizardly men, who went here and there, seeming to do little and say less.

"I think they're hunting for a new archmage after all," said Tenar.

"Or looking for abuses of the art," Ged said—"sorcery gone wrong."

Tenar was going to say, "Then they should look

in the manor house of Re Albi!" but her tongue stumbled on the words. What was I going to say? she thought. Did I ever tell Ged about— I'm getting forgetful. What was it I was going to tell Ged? Oh, that we'd better mend the lower pasture gate before the cows get out.

There was always something, a dozen things, in the front of her mind, business of the farm. "Never one thing, for you," Ogion had said. Even with Ged to help her, all her thoughts and days went into the business of the farm. He shared the housework with her as Flint had not; but Flint had been a farmer, and Ged was not. He learned fast, but there was a lot to learn. They worked. There was little time for talk, now. At the day's end there was supper together, and bed together, and sleep, and wake at dawn and back to work, and so round and so round, like the wheel of a water mill, rising full and emptying, the days like the bright water falling.

"Hello, mother," said the thin fellow at the farmyard gate. She thought it was Lark's eldest and said, "What brings you by, lad?" Then she looked back at him across the clucking chickens and the parading geese.

"Spark!" she cried, and scattered the poultry, running to him.

"Well, well," he said. "Don't carry on."

He let her embrace him and stroke his face. He came in and sat down in the kitchen, at the table.

"Have you eaten? Did you see Apple?"

"I could eat."

She rummaged in the well-stocked larder. "What ship are you on? Still the *Gull?*"

"No." A pause. "My ship's broke up."

She turned in horror—"Wrecked?"

"No." He smiled without humor. "Crew's broke up. King's men took her over."

"But—it wasn't a pirate ship—"

"No."

"Then why—?"

"Said the captain was running some goods they wanted," he said, unwillingly. He was as thin as ever, but looked older, tanned dark, lank-haired, with a long, narrow face like Flint's but still narrower, harder.

"Where's dad?" he said.

Tenar stood still.

"You didn't stop by your sister's."

"No," he said, indifferent.

"Flint died three years ago," she said. "Of a stroke. In the fields—on the path up from the lambing pens. Clearbrook found him. It was three years ago."

There was a silence. He did not know what to say, or had nothing to say.

She put food before him. He began to eat so hungrily that she set out more at once.

"When did you eat last?"

He shrugged, and ate.

She sat down across the table from him. Late-spring sunshine poured in the low window across the table and shone on the brass fender in the hearth.

He pushed the plate away at last.

"So who's been running the farm?" he asked.

"What's that to you, son?" she asked him, gently but drily.

"It's mine," he said, in a rather similar tone.

After a minute Tenar got up and cleared his dishes away. "So it is."

"You can stay, o' course," he said, very awkwardly, perhaps attempting to joke; but he was not a joking man. "Old Clearbrook still around?"

"They're all still here. And a man called Hawk, and a child I keep. Here. In the house. You'll have to sleep in the loft-room. I'll put the ladder up." She faced him again. "Are you here for a stay, then?"

"I might be."

So Flint had answered her questions for twenty years, denying her right to ask them by never answering yes or no, maintaining a freedom based on her ignorance; a poor, narrow sort of freedom, she thought.

"Poor lad," she said, "your crew broken up, and your father dead, and strangers in your house, all in a day. You'll want some time to get used to it all. I'm sorry, my son. But I'm glad you're here. I thought of you often, on the seas, in the storms, in winter."

He said nothing. He had nothing to offer, and was unable to accept. He pushed back his chair and was about to get up when Therru came in. He stared, half-risen—"What happened to her?" he said.

"She was burned. Here's my son I told you about, Therru, the sailor, Spark. Therru's your sister, Spark."

"Sister!"

"By adoption."

"Sister!" he said again, and looked around the kitchen as if for witness, and stared at his mother.

She stared back.

He went out, going wide of Therru, who stood motionless. He slammed the door behind him.

Tenar started to speak to Therru and could not.

"Don't cry," said the child who did not cry, coming to her, touching her arm. "Did he hurt you?"

"Oh Therru! Let me hold you!" She sat down at the table with Therru on her lap and in her arms, though the girl was getting big to be held, and had never learned how to do it easily. But Tenar held her and wept, and Therru bent her scarred face down against Tenar's, till it was wet with tears.

Ged and Spark came in at dusk from opposite ends of the farm. Spark had evidently talked with Clearbrook and thought the situation over, and Ged was evidently trying to size it up. Very little was said at supper, and that cautiously. Spark made no complaint about not having his own room back, but ran up the ladder to the storage-loft like the sailor he was, and was apparently satisfied with the bed his mother had made him there, for he did not come back down till late in the morning.

He wanted breakfast then, and expected it to be served to him. His father had always been waited on by mother, wife, daughter. Was he less a man than his father? Was she to prove it to him? She served him his meal and cleared it away for him, and went back to the orchard where she and Therru and Shandy were burning off a plague of tent caterpillars that threatened to destroy the new-set fruit.

Spark went off to join Clearbrook and Tiff. And he stayed mostly with them, as the days passed. The heavy work requiring muscle and the skilled work with crops and sheep was done by Ged, Shandy, and Tenar, while the two old men who had been there all their lives, his father's men, took him about and told him how they managed it all, and truly believed they were managing it all, and shared their belief with him.

Tenar became miserable in the house. Only outdoors, at the farmwork, did she have relief from the anger, the shame that Spark's presence brought her.

"My turn," she said to Ged, bitterly, in the starlit darkness of their room. "My turn to lose what I was proudest of."

"What have you lost?"

"My son. The son I did not bring up to be a man.

I failed. I failed him." She bit her lip, gazing dry-eyed into the dark.

Ged did not try to argue with her or persuade her out of her grief. He asked, "Do you think he'll stay?"

"Yes. He's afraid to try and go back to sea. He didn't tell me the truth, or not all the truth, about his ship. He was second mate. I suppose he was involved in carrying stolen goods. Secondhand piracy. I don't care. Gontish sailors are all half-pirate. But he lies about it. He lies. He is jealous of you. A dishonest, envious man."

"Frightened, I think," Ged said. "Not wicked. And it is his farm."

"Then he can have it! And may it be as generous to him as—"

"No, dear love," Ged said, catching her with both voice and hands—"don't speak—don't say the evil word!" He was so urgent, so passionately earnest, that her anger turned right about into the love that was its source, and she cried, "I wouldn't curse him, or this place! I didn't mean it! Only it makes me so sorry, so ashamed! I am so sorry, Ged!"

"No, no, no. My dear, I don't care what the boy thinks of me. But he's very hard on you."

"And Therru. He treats her like— He said, he said to me, 'What did she do, to look like that?' What did *she do*—!"

Ged stroked her hair, as he often did, with a light, slow, repeated caress that would make them both sleepy with loving pleasure.

"I could go off goat-herding again," he said at last. "It would make things easier for you here. Except for the work. . . ."

"I'd rather come with you."

He stroked her hair, and seemed to be considering. "I suppose we might," he said. "There were a couple of families up there sheep-herding, above Lissu. But then comes the winter. . . ."

"Maybe some farmer would take us on. I know the work—and sheep—and you know goats—and you're quick at everything—"

"Useful with pitchforks," he murmured, and got a little sob of a laugh from her.

The next morning Spark was up early to breakfast with them, for he was going fishing with old Tiff. He got up from the table, saying with a better grace than usual, "I'll bring a mess of fish for supper."

Tenar had made resolves overnight. She said, "Wait; you can clear off the table, Spark. Set the dishes in the sink and put water on 'em. They'll be washed with the supper things."

He stared a moment and said, "That's women's work," putting on his cap.

"It's anybody's work who eats in this kitchen."

"Not mine," he said flatly, and went out.

She followed him. She stood on the doorstep. "Hawk's, but not yours?" she demanded.

He merely nodded, going on across the yard.

"It's too late," she said, turning back to the

kitchen. "Failed, failed." She could feel the lines in her face, stiff, beside the mouth, between the eyes. "You can water a stone," she said, "but it won't grow."

"You have to start when they're young and tender," Ged said. "Like me."

This time she couldn't laugh.

They came back to the house from the day's work and saw a man talking with Spark at the front gate.

"That's the fellow from Re Albi, isn't it?" said Ged, whose eyes were very good.

"Come along, Therru," Tenar said, for the child had stopped short. "What fellow?" She was rather nearsighted, and squinted across the yard. "Oh, it's what's his name, the sheep-dealer. Townsend. What's he back here for, the carrion crow!"

Her mood all day had been fierce, and Ged and Therru wisely said nothing.

She went to the men at the gate.

"Did you come about the ewe lambs, Townsend? You're a year late; but there's some of this year's yet in the fold."

"So the master's been telling me," said Townsend.

"Has he," said Tenar.

Spark's face went darker than ever at her tone.

"I won't interrupt you and the master, then," said she, and was turning away when Townsend spoke: "I've got a message for you, Goha."

"Third time's the charm."

"The old witch, you know, old Moss, she's in a

bad way. She said, since I was coming down to Middle Valley, she said, 'Tell Mistress Goha I'd like to see her before I die, if there's a chance of her coming.'"

Crow, carrion crow, Tenar thought, looking with hatred at the bearer of bad news.

"She's ill?"

"Sick to death," Townsend said, with a kind of smirk that might be intended for sympathy. "Took sick in the winter, and she's failing fast, and so she said to tell you she wants bad to see you, before she dies."

"Thank you for bringing the message," Tenar said soberly, and turned to go to the house. Townsend went on with Spark to the sheepfolds.

As they prepared dinner, Tenar said to Ged and Therru, "I must go."

"Of course," Ged said. "The three of us, if you like."

"Would you?" For the first time that day her face lightened, the storm cloud lifted. "Oh," she said, "that's—that's good—I didn't want to ask, I thought maybe— Therru, would you like to go back to the little house, Ogion's house, for a while?"

Therru stood still to think. "I could see my peach tree," she said.

"Yes, and Heather—and Sippy—and Moss— poor Moss! Oh, I have longed, I have longed to go back up there, but it didn't seem right. There was the farm to run—and all—"

It seemed to her that there was some other reason she had not gone back, had not let herself think of going back, had not even known till now that she yearned to go; but whatever the reason was it slipped away like a shadow, a word forgotten. "Has anyone looked after Moss, I wonder, did anyone send for a healer. She's the only healer on the Overfell, but there's people down in Gont Port who could help her, surely. Oh, poor Moss! I want to go— It's too late, but tomorrow, tomorrow early. And the master can make his own breakfast!"

"He'll learn," said Ged.

"No, he won't. He'll find some fool woman to do it for him. Ah!" She looked around the kitchen, her face bright and fierce. "I hate to leave her the twenty years I've scoured that table. I hope she appreciates it!"

Spark brought Townsend in for supper, but the sheep-dealer would not stay the night, though he was of course offered a bed in common hospitality. It would have been one of their beds, and Tenar did not like the thought. She was glad to see him go off to his hosts in the village in the blue twilight of the spring evening.

"We'll be off to Re Albi first thing tomorrow, son," she said to Spark. "Hawk and Therru and I."

He looked a little frightened.

"Just go off like that?"

"So you went; so you came," said his mother.

"Now look here, Spark: this is your father's money-box. There's seven ivory pieces in it, and those credit counters from old Bridgeman, but he'll never pay, he hasn't got anything to pay with. These four Andradean pieces Flint got from selling sheepskins to the ship's outfitter in Valmouth four years running, back when you were a boy. These three Havnorian ones are what Tholy paid us for the High Creek farm. I had your father buy that farm, and I helped him clear it and sell it. I'll take those three pieces, for I've earned them. The rest, and the farm, is yours. You're the master." The tall, thin young man stood there with his gaze on the money-box.

"Take it all. I don't want it," he said in a low voice.

"I don't need it. But I thank you, my son. Keep the four pieces. When you marry, call them my gift to your wife."

She put the box away in the place behind the big plate on the top shelf of the dresser, where Flint had always kept it. "Therru, get your things ready now, because we'll go very early."

"When are you coming back?" Spark asked, and the tone of his voice made Tenar think of the restless, frail child he had been. But she said only, "I don't know, my dear. If you need me, I'll come."

She busied herself getting out their travel shoes and packs. "Spark," she said, "you can do something for me."

He had sat down in the hearthseat, looking uncertain and morose. "What?"

"Go down to Valmouth, soon, and see your sister. And tell her that I've gone back to the Overfell. Tell her, if she wants me, just send word."

He nodded. He watched Ged, who had already packed his few belongings with the neatness and dispatch of one who had traveled much, and was now putting up the dishes to leave the kitchen in good order. That done, he sat down opposite Spark to run a new cord through the eyelets of his pack to close it at the top.

"There's a knot they use for that," Spark said. "Sailor's knot."

Ged silently handed the pack across the hearth, and watched as Spark silently demonstrated the knot.

"Slips up, see," he said, and Ged nodded.

They left the farm in the dark and cold of the morning. Sunlight comes late to the western side of Gont Mountain, and only walking kept them warm till at last the sun got round the great mass of the south peak and shone on their backs.

Therru was twice the walker she had been the summer before, but it was still a two days' journey for them. Along in the afternoon, Tenar asked, "Shall we try to get on to Oak Springs today? There's a sort of inn. We had a cup of milk there, remember, Therru?"

Ged was looking up the mountainside with a far-away expression. "There's a place I know. . . ."

"Fine," said Tenar.

A little before they came to the high corner of the road from which Gont Port could first be seen, Ged turned aside from the road into the forest that covered the steep slopes above it. The westering sun sent slanting red-gold rays into the darkness between the trunks and under the branches. They climbed half a mile or so, on no path Tenar could see, and came out on a little step or shelf of the mountainside, a meadow sheltered from the wind by the cliffs behind it and the trees about it. From there one could see the heights of the mountain to the north, and between the tops of great firs there was one clear view of the western sea. It was entirely silent there except when the wind breathed in the firs. One mountain lark sang long and sweet, away up in the sunlight, before dropping to her nest in the untrodden grass.

The three of them ate their bread and cheese. They watched darkness rise up the mountain from the sea. They made their bed of cloaks and slept, Therru next to Tenar next to Ged. In the deep night Tenar woke. An owl was calling nearby, a sweet repeated note like a bell, and far off up the mountain its mate replied like the ghost of a bell. Tenar thought, "I'll watch the stars set in the sea," but she fell asleep again at once in peace of heart.

She woke in the grey morning to see Ged sitting

up beside her, his cloak pulled round his shoulders, looking out through the gap westward. His dark face was quite still, full of silence, as she had seen it once long ago on the beach of Atuan. His eyes were not downcast, as then; he looked into the illimitable west. Looking with him she saw the day coming, the glory of rose and gold reflected clear across the sky.

He turned to her, and she said to him, "I have loved you since I first saw you."

"Life-giver," he said and leaned forward, kissing her breast and mouth. She held him a moment. They got up, and waked Therru, and went on their way; but as they entered the trees Tenar looked back once at the little meadow as if charging it to keep faith with her happiness there.

The first day of the journey their goal had been journeying. This day they would come to Re Albi. So Tenar's mind was much on Aunty Moss, wondering what had befallen her and whether she was indeed dying. But as the day and the way went on her mind would not hold to the thought of Moss, or any thought. She was tired. She did not like walking this way again to death. They passed Oak Springs, and went down into the gorge, and started up again. By the last long uphill stretch to the Overfell, her legs were hard to lift, and her mind was stupid and confused, fastening upon one word or image until it became meaningless—the dish-cupboard in Ogion's house, or the words *bone dolphin,* which came into her head from seeing Therru's grass bag of toys, and repeated themselves endlessly.

Ged strode along at his easy traveler's gait, and Therru trudged right beside him, the same Therru who had worn out on this long climb less than a year ago, and had to be carried. But that had been after a longer day of walking. And the child had still been recovering from her punishment.

She was getting old, too old to walk so far so fast. It was so hard going uphill. An old woman should stay home by her fireside. The bone dolphin, the bone dolphin. Bone, bound, the binding spell. The bone man and the bone animal. There they went ahead. They were waiting for her. She was slow. She was tired. She toiled on up the last stretch of the hill and came up to them where the road came out on the level of the Overfell. To the left were the roofs of Re Albi slanting down towards the cliff's edge. To the right the road went up to the manor house. "This way," Tenar said.

"No," the child said, pointing left, to the village.

"This way," Tenar repeated, and set off on the right-hand way. Ged came with her.

They walked between the walnut orchards and the fields of grass. It was a warm late afternoon of early summer. Birds sang in the orchard trees near and far. He came walking down the road from the great house towards them, the one whose name she could not remember.

"Welcome!" he said, and stopped, smiling at them.

They stopped.

"What great personages have come to honor the house of the Lord of Re Albi," he said. Tuaho, that was not his name. The bone dolphin, the bone animal, the bone child.

"My Lord Archmage!" He bowed low, and Ged bowed to him.

"And my Lady Tenar of Atuan!" He bowed even lower to her, and she got down on her knees in the road. Her head sank down, till she put her hands in the dirt and crouched until her mouth too was on the dirt of the road.

"Now crawl," he said, and she began to crawl towards him.

"Stop," he said, and she stopped.

"Can you talk?" he asked. She said nothing, having no words that would come to her mouth, but Ged replied in his usual quiet voice, "Yes."

"Where's the monster?"

"I don't know."

"I thought the witch would bring her familiar with her. But she brought you instead. The Lord Archmage Sparrowhawk. What a splendid substitute! All I can do to witches and monsters is cleanse the world of them. But to you, who used at one time to be a man, I can talk; you are capable of rational speech, at least. And capable of understanding punishment. You thought you were safe, I suppose, with your king on the throne, and my master, our master, destroyed. You thought you'd had your will, and destroyed the promise of eternal life, didn't you?"

"No," said Ged's voice.

She could not see them. She could see only the dirt of the road, and taste it her mouth. She heard Ged speak. He said, "In dying is life."

"Quack, quack, quote the Songs, Master of Roke—schoolmaster! What a funny sight to see, the great archmage all got up like a goatherd, and not an ounce of magic in him—not a word of power. Can you say a spell, archmage? Just a little spell—just a tiny charm of illusion? No? Not a word? My master defeated you. Now do you know it? You did not conquer him. His power lives! I might keep you alive here awhile, to see that power—my power. To see the old man I keep from death—and I might use your life for that if I need it—and to see your meddling king make a fool of himself, with his mincing lords and stupid wizards, looking for a woman! A woman to rule us! But the rule is here, the mastery is here, here, in this house. All this year I've been gathering others to me, men who know the true power. From Roke, some of them, from right under the noses of the school-masters. And from Havnor, from under the nose of that so-called Son of Morred, who wants a woman to rule him, your king who thinks he's so safe he can go by his true name. Do you know my name, archmage? Do you remember me, four years ago, when you were the great Master of Masters and I was a lowly student at Roke?"

"You were called Aspen," said the patient voice.

"And my true name?"

"I don't know your true name."

"What? You don't know it? Can't you find it? Don't mages know all names?"

"I'm not a mage."

"Oh, say it again."

"I'm not a mage."

"I like to hear you say it. Say it again."

"I'm not a mage."

"But I am!"

"Yes."

"Say it!"

"You are a mage."

"Ah! This is better than I hoped! I fished for the eel and caught the whale! Come on, then, come meet my friends. You can walk. She can crawl."

So they went up the road to the manor house of the Lord of Re Albi and went in, Tenar on hands and knees on the road, and on the marble steps up to the door, and on the marble pavements of the halls and rooms.

Inside the house it was dark. With the darkness came a darkness into Tenar's mind, so that she understood less and less of what was said. Only some words and voices came to her clearly. What Ged said she understood, and when he spoke she thought of his name, and clung to it in her mind. But he spoke very seldom, and only to answer the one whose name was not Tuaho. That one spoke to her now and then, calling her Bitch. "This is my new pet," he said to other men, several of them that were there in the darkness where candles made shadows. "See how well trained she is? Roll over, Bitch!" She rolled over, and the men laughed.

"She had a whelp," he said, "that I planned to finish punishing, since it was left half-burned. But she brought me a bird she'd caught instead, a sparrowhawk. Tomorrow we'll teach it to fly."

Other voices said words, but she did not understand words any more.

Something was fastened around her neck and she was made to crawl up more stairs and into a room that smelled of urine and rotting meat and sweet flowers. Voices spoke. A cold hand like a stone struck her head feebly while something laughed, "Eh, eh, eh," like an old door creaking back and forth. Then she was kicked and made to crawl down halls. She could not crawl fast enough, and was kicked in the breasts and in the mouth. Then there was a door that crashed, and silence, and the dark. She heard somebody crying and thought it was the child, her child. She wanted the child not to cry. At last it stopped.

TEHANU

THE CHILD TURNED LEFT AND WENT SOME way before she looked back, letting the blossoming hedgerow hide her.

The one called Aspen, whose name was Erisen, and whom she saw as a forked and writhing darkness, had bound her mother and father, with a thong through her tongue and a thong through his heart, and was leading them up toward the place where he hid. The smell of the place was sickening to her, but she followed a little way to see what he did. He led them in and shut the door behind them. It was a stone door. She could not enter there.

She needed to fly, but she could not fly; she was not one of the winged ones.

She ran as fast as she could across the fields, past

Aunty Moss's house, past Ogion's house and the goats' house, onto the path along the cliff and to the edge of the cliff, where she was not to go because she could see it only with one eye. She was careful. She looked carefully with that eye. She stood on the edge. The water was far below, and the sun was setting far away. She looked into the west with the other eye, and called with the other voice the name she had heard in her mother's dream.

She did not wait for an answer, but turned round again and went back—first past Ogion's house to see if her peach tree had grown. The old tree stood bearing many small, green peaches, but there was no sign of the seedling. The goats had eaten it. Or it had died because she had not watered it. She stood a little while looking at the ground there, then drew a long breath and went on back across the fields to Aunty Moss's house.

Chickens going to roost squawked and fluttered, protesting her entrance. The little hut was dark and very full of smells. "Aunty Moss?" she said, in the voice she had for these people.

"Who's there?"

The old woman was in her bed, hiding. She was frightened, and tried to make stone around her to keep everyone away, but it didn't work; she was not strong enough.

"Who is it? Who's there? Oh dearie—oh dearie child, my little burned one, my pretty, what are you doing here? Where's she, where's she, your mother, oh, is she here? Did she come? Don't come in, don't come in, dearie, there's a curse on me, he cursed the old woman, don't come near me! Don't come near!"

She wept. The child put out her hand and touched her. "You're cold," she said.

"You're like fire, child, your hand burns me. Oh, don't look at me! He made my flesh rot, and shrivel, and rot again, but he won't let me die—he said I'd bring you here. I tried to die, I tried, but he held me, he held me living against my will, he won't let me die, oh, let me die!"

"You shouldn't die," the child said, frowning.

"Child," the old woman whispered, "dearie—call me by my name."

"Hatha," the child said.

"Ah. I knew. . . . Set me free, dearie!"

"I have to wait," the child said. "Till they come."

The witch lay easier, breathing without pain. "Till who come, dearie?" she whispered.

"My people."

The witch's big, cold hand lay like a bundle of sticks in hers. She held it firmly. It was as dark now outside the hut as inside it. Hatha, who was called Moss, slept; and presently the child, sitting on the floor beside her cot, with a hen perched nearby, slept also.

Men came when the light came. He said, "Up, Bitch! Up!" She got to her hands and knees. He laughed, saying, "All the way up! You're a clever bitch, you can walk on your hind legs, can't you? That's it. Pretend to be human! We have a way to go now. Come!" The strap was still around her neck, and he jerked it. She followed him.

"Here, you lead her," he said, and now it was that one, the one she loved, but she did not know his name any more, who held the strap.

They all came out of the dark place. Stone yawned to let them pass and ground together behind them.

He was always close beside her and the one who held the strap. Others came behind, three or four men.

The fields were grey with dew. The mountain was dark against a pale sky. Birds were beginning to sing in the orchards and hedgerows, louder and louder.

They came to the edge of the world and walked along it for a while until they came to where the ground was only rock and the edge was very narrow. There was a line in the rock, and she looked at that.

"He can push her," he said. "And then the hawk can fly, all by himself."

He unfastened the strap from around her neck.

"Go stand at the edge," he said. She followed the mark in the stone out to the edge. The sea was below her, nothing else. The air was out beyond her.

"Now, Sparrowhawk will give her a push," he

said. "But first, maybe she wants to say something. She has so much to say. Women always do. Isn't there anything you'd like to say to us, Lady Tenar?"

She could not speak, but she pointed to the sky above the sea.

"Albatross," he said.

She laughed aloud.

In the gulfs of light, from the doorway of the sky, the dragon flew, fire trailing behind the coiling, mailed body. Tenar spoke then.

"Kalessin!" she cried, and then turned, seizing Ged's arm, pulling him down to the rock, as the roar of fire went over them, the rattle of mail and the hiss of wind in upraised wings, the clash of the talons like scytheblades on the rock.

The wind blew from the sea. A tiny thistle growing in a cleft in the rock near her hand nodded and nodded in the wind from the sea.

Ged was beside her. They were crouched side by side, the sea behind them and the dragon before them.

It looked at them sidelong from one long, yellow eye.

Ged spoke in a hoarse, shaking voice, in the dragon's language. Tenar understood the words, which were only, "Our thanks, Eldest."

Looking at Tenar, Kalessin spoke, in the huge voice like a broom of metal dragged across a gong: *"Aro Tehanu?"*

"The child," Tenar said—"Therru!" She got to

her feet to run, to seek her child. She saw her coming along the ledge of rock between the mountain and the sea, toward the dragon.

"Don't run, Therru!" she cried, but the child had seen her and was running, running straight to her. They clung to each other.

The dragon turned its enormous, rust-dark head to watch them with both eyes. The nostril pits, big as kettles, were bright with fire, and wisps of smoke curled from them. The heat of the dragon's body beat through the cold sea wind.

"Tehanu," the dragon said.

The child turned to look at it.

"Kalessin," she said.

Then Ged, who had remained kneeling, stood up, though shakily, catching Tenar's arm to steady himself. He laughed. "Now I know who called thee, Eldest!" he said.

"I did," the child said. "I did not know what else to do, Segoy."

She still looked at the dragon, and she spoke in the language of the dragons, the words of the Making.

"It was well, child," the dragon said. "I have sought thee long."

"Shall we go there now?" the child asked. "Where the others are, on the other wind?"

"Would you leave these?"

"No," said the child. "Can they not come?"

"They cannot come. Their life is here."

"I will stay with them," she said, with a little catch of breath.

Kalessin turned aside to give that immense furnace-blast of laughter or contempt or delight or anger—"Hah!" Then, looking again at the child, "It is well. Thou hast work to do here."

"I know," the child said.

"I will come back for thee," Kalessin said, "in time." And, to Ged and Tenar, "I give you my child, as you will give me yours."

"In time," Tenar said.

Kalessin's great head bowed very slightly, and the long, sword-toothed mouth curled up at the corner.

Ged and Tenar drew aside with Therru as the dragon turned, dragging its armor across the ledge, placing its taloned feet carefully, gathering its black haunches like a cat, till it sprang aloft. The vaned wings shot up crimson in the new light, the spurred tail rang hissing on the rock, and it flew, it was gone—a gull, a swallow, a thought.

Where it had been lay scorched rags of cloth and leather, and other things.

"Come away," Ged said.

But the woman and the child stood and looked at those things.

"They are bone people," Therru said. She turned away then and set off. She went ahead of the man and woman along the narrow path.

"Her native tongue," Ged said. "Her mother tongue."

"Tehanu," said Tenar. "Her name is Tehanu."

"She has been given it by the giver of names."

"She has been Tehanu since the beginning. Always, she has been Tehanu."

"Come on!" the child said, looking back at them. "Aunty Moss is sick."

They were able to move Moss out into the light and air, to wash her sores, and to burn the foul linens of her bed, while Therru brought clean bedding from Ogion's house. She also brought Heather the goatgirl back with her. With Heather's help they got the old woman comfortable in her bed, with her chickens; and Heather promised to come back with something for them to eat.

"Someone must go down to Gont Port," Ged said, "for the wizard there. To look after Moss; she can be healed. And to go to the manor house. The old man will die now. The grandson might live, if the house is made clean. . . ." He had sat down on the doorstep of Moss's house. He leaned his head back against the doorjamb, in the sunlight, and closed his eyes. "Why do we do what we do?" he said.

Tenar was washing her face and hands and arms in a basin of clear water she had drawn from the pump. She looked round when she was done. Utterly spent, Ged had fallen asleep, his face a little upturned to the morning light. She sat down beside him on the doorstep and laid her head against his shoulder. Are we spared? she thought. How is it we are spared?

She looked down at Ged's hand, relaxed and open on the earthen step. She thought of the thistle that nodded in the wind, and of the taloned foot of the dragon with its scales of red and gold. She was half-asleep when the child sat down beside her.

"Tehanu," she murmured.

"The little tree died," the child said.

After a while Tenar's weary, sleepy mind understood, and woke up enough to make a reply. "Are there peaches on the old tree?"

They spoke low, not to waken the sleeping man.

"Only little green ones."

"They'll ripen, after the Long Dance. Soon now."

"Can we plant one?"

"More than one, if you like. Is the house all right?"

"It's empty."

"Shall we live there?" She roused a little more, and put her arm around the child. "I have money," she said, "enough to buy a herd of goats, and Turby's winter-pasture, if it's still for sale. Ged knows where to take them up the mountain, summers. . . . I wonder if the wool we combed is still there?" So saying, she thought, We left the books, Ogion's books! On the mantel at Oak Farm—for Spark, poor boy, he can't read a word of them!

But it did not seem to matter. There were new things to be learned, no doubt. And she could send somebody for the books, if Ged wanted them. And for her spinning wheel. Or she could go down herself, come autumn, and see her son, and visit with Lark, and stay a while with Apple. They would have to replant Ogion's garden right away if they wanted any vegetables of their own this summer. She thought of the rows of beans and the scent of the bean flowers. She thought of the small window that looked west. "I think we can live there," she said.